The Cuban Conne

An Adventure Novel

By

J.T.S. Brown

Table of Contents

The Cuban Connection

The Cuban Connection: A Stephen Masters Adventure

Chapter 1
THE MEMORY OF IT

The plane was the smallest jet in the typical menu of those for selection by major airlines in the mid 1980's. With good reason. How often does one need a huge, wide body jet at Harrisburg International? The flight to Miami, Florida involved only one stop, which was to be at Atlanta. It was nice to attend the Industrial Relations Conference in a place like Miami Beach. In that subject area of concern, they are normally held in more labor intensive cities like Detroit, Atlanta, Chicago, New York, or in cities of political influence like Washington, D.C.

My body was still somewhat in revolt from a rough night before.

It's often hard as a single public official to cut loose and have fun. But, I manage. Last night it was in a little town called Carlisle, Pennsylvania, near the capital. I dated a lady Major stationed at the War College in Carlisle. Probably it would be more accurate to say she dated me. She was a career officer, married to the Army. I felt like a sex object for the first time in years. She ran the whole show from ordering dinner to what position in bed and in what order. A lovely girl, but a little too strong in the personality area. Not that I'm a male dominant type, the truth is, it's almost the opposite. But, I prefer sharing the love making chores in a more intimate climate.

My mind continued to drift thinking about her. God, was she in great shape physically. Must be all the marching or whatever. It was all I could do to keep up with her. I vowed to do more sit-ups to get in better shape before seeing her again.

"Hello, Mr. Secretary, what's your business going to be in Atlanta?"

"Well, it's good to see the airline didn't abandon us in Pennsylvania to less than beautiful flight attendants. I'm a speaker at a conference in Miami Beach. The first time for me to speak to this group, and, rather nervous about it I might say."

"We'll fix you up with a couple of stiff drinks. If I remember correctly, you like rye whiskey and soda. We still don't carry rye whiskey on this route. How about a good Irish whiskey?"

"How do you remember I like rye whiskey? I fly a lot, but certainly not that much."

"You're the only one who has ever consistently asked for it. Besides, you're a local political figure in Harrisburg and the state. Put the two together and it's easy. Have you been to Miami recently?"

"No, Leslie, not recently." It was almost a melancholy answer without any substance to the voice behind the words. I stared out the window of the plane and dreamed of times past that were spent in the neighboring cities of Miami and Miami Beach.

I remembered the drive through Miami Beach along Collins Avenue starting at the old South Beach area, where the poor elderly Jews live, many of them surviving on cat food and fruit. What a way to spend one's golden years. But the whole city was like that; dramatic evidence of how down and out the poor could be and how lofty the rich could become.

The blacks were in Miami, not many by comparison to New York or Washington. The black sections of poverty in Miami were spread in various parts of the city. One section was somewhat of a contrast that fascinated everyone from the ordinary visitor to the research sociologist. On the fringe of Miami and Coral Gables, situated between Coconut Grove, there was a pocket of black poverty as bad as any to be witnessed. The Grove, as it's called, and the "Gables" are posh wealthy communities nestled in the Miami metro complex, separated only by U.S. 1 and a strip of black poverty.

I lived in New York City for a while. The rich knew how to be rich there. They have a sort of class. They may go to fancy restaurants and plays, but they're not as conspicuous about every single aspect of their lives. Palm Beach, Miami, Coral Gables, Key Biscayne, and Florida in general, all lack class when it comes to wealth. The overt conspicuous consumption makes them seem like cheap whore houses. In these places, everything from their homes to their graves are gaudy. For brief visits, it's fun and exciting. When I lived and worked there, I felt like a prostitute. It was hard to live among starving old people, poor blacks, and immigrant Latin's in a posh environment and not feel guilty. Leaving helped rid my conscience of at least that much anguish.

My deep thoughts were disturbed by a soft Spanish accent. My seat partner next to the aisle was a beautiful woman with dark hair and eyes so dark they looked black. Her outfit certainly didn't do anything to accent her beauty. God, what she must look like in a seductive outfit. She wore a drab gray-looking suit and plain black boots with an off-white blouse and little jewelry to speak of.

She was a tall Latin, long legs, well-proportioned with full breasts. My mind went wild. I could envision a seduction next to none with she and I happy participants. That beautiful dark hair and tan world look so lovely against the backdrop of white silk sheets. Spending a long time just holding the young naked body next to mine, necking like two experimenting high school kids who discovered how it feels to kiss. LORD!! Followed up by a slow and beautiful lovemaking. Afterward, sipping champagne in the tub together before going out to dinner.

If she only knew what a great dream she was missing. Too bad mental telepathy isn't possible. I'd either be slapped or enjoying the greatest night of my life in Miami.

"Are you okay sir?"

I responded with a less than elegant or witty "yes". My God, I'm still a half-step slow with women in my mid-thirties. The long gape at how lovely she was, combined with coming out of a deep fantasy must be the excuse. I hope!

"Yes, I was just daydreaming. Sorry, very rude of me. My name is Stephen Masters, and yours?"

"Joyce, Joyce Hurtado. I wasn't trying to bother you. Other than you're sort of sitting on a magazine I want to read. I heard the stewardess mention you're going to Miami to a conference. Thank you for the magazine."

"You're welcome. I'm speaking at a labor conference. My area of work is in that line."

"I'm sorry, I do know that. You're the Secretary of Labor for the State of Pennsylvania. j-was supposed to be at a presentation you made at State College, but I couldn't make the plane connection between Pittsburgh and Harrisburg."

"You didn't miss a great deal, I'm afraid. The discussion broke down to debates over state budget cuts in education by the Governor and the Department of Education in Washington. A lot of kids have lost or are losing their student guaranteed loans and grants. Are you the Cuban diplomat who Was sent over when relations began to be normalized again? I've seen your picture before. It's coming back to me now that we've talked."

"Yes, I have the privilege of being one of Fidel's representatives to serve the people of my country. I have a real good understanding of America and her people. I went to school here in Pennsylvania at State College."

"Why would you attend school in America, in lieu of a country more in tune with your political and economic philosophies?"

"Aren't we being a bit provincial with that question? The academic community in America is not a sales forum for democracy. It's neutral to liberal at best, and some professors are more radical than any group in Habana. Besides, there are those of us who are loyal to Cuba, not necessarily the Communists, and feel our presence helps keep some hope alive that Cuba will be turned away from political and military destruction."

"It must be very difficult for you. I know I get excited about conditions of unrest here, and we, in theory, have a democracy."

"Isn't it politically dangerous to be candid in your comments in America?"

"Yes, but you're not a reporter. Any statements about me coming from you would be taken as slander."

-------- -------- -------- ---

"Ladies and gentlemen, this plane is being taken in the name of El Movimiento Nueavo Political. (The new political movement). No one will be harmed if you pay attention and do as you're instructed.

"Friends of yours I presume?"

"No, Steve, they are a radical group; anti-Castro, but not aligned with the U.S. either. They are a revolutionary movement, dedicated to a militant introduction of Marxism to our hemisphere."

"It would seem the Cuban population in America might be behind them."

"No, they find them too radical. I don't know how they took over the plane, and why a Harrisburg flight."

"Security in Harrisburg isn't the tightest, especially for hijackings to Cuba. We don't have much of that sort of thing in the Bible belt. But you're correct, the security would have picked up the weapons at least."

"Well, if they're not friends of yours, Joyce, you may be the reason for this. Looks like we're to find out soon enough; here come one of them."

"Up front please, both of you."

The funny looking weapons they carried were shoved in our faces. Joyce stood quickly and started to move forward. I was yanked by the tie to the plane aisle. The process was most undignified, so was the shove to get me toward the front of the plane. Our walk to the front of the plane and the standing there waiting to find out what they wanted seemed forever. My right lower leg was moving in an uncontrollable twitch, sort of like when I gave my first presentation in tenth grade speech class. I knew I had to say something or fall apart slowly by twitching to death.

"Impatient group aren't they? Why did they shove us up here?"

"This is a radical group that uses violence. Don't antagonize them, Steve."

"Violence? You said radical before. That's a big word to leave out. I wouldn't have been so flippant."

"We didn't count on your being on this plane Secretary Masters, only Miss Hurtado. What a plus! We are taking the plane to Cuba."

"You can't land this plane in Habana with all these passengers and yourselves. My government will arrest your group."

"Quiet Miss Hurtado, we have no intention of taking all the people there. They will be let out in Atlanta. Only you and the Secretary are going to Cuba.

"Excuse me, but if you don't need me I'll be happy to get off in Atlanta with the others and give a full report of what you wish said to the press. I'm in no way connected to international politics. In fact, I've never heard of your group before today."

"Secretary Masters, don't you read today's papers? We are the ones responsible for the bomb blast across from the U.N. yesterday afternoon. And yes, you are involved. You write and speak of labor unrest. We also have sympathy with labor unrest."

"Mine is of a domestic note; bad management with lack of proper foresight that blames its poor productivity and unreliable engineering designs on workers. Not the political overtures you speak of now."

"Pardon the interruption, Steve, but you..."

"My name is Perez Guerra, Miss Hurtado."

"Okay, but you said drop off the passengers. No mention was made of where you will land in Cuba. You're wanted here and in Cuba. What makes you think you can land a plane this big at an airfield without being caught?"

"Companera, we have engineered this whole plan in a masterful way. We brought the parts of the weapons on board the plane as trinkets on neck chains, jacket and boot zippers, and parts of belt buckles and in the lead bags used for film protection. We assembled them in the toilet once on board. With no one even remotely figuring out what we were doing. Juan is in with the captain giving him instructions on what to do and I am here with two other helpers in the plane."

"Harrisburg Airport was selected because of its location from New York and its easy accessibility. With all the Cuban and Vietnamese refugees near there, people are not unaccustomed to seeing a group of Latins or foreigners.

"We drove to Harrisburg in two cars by separate routes. One by the Interstate Route across the state from New York City, the other group down New Jersey to Philadelphia and across Route 30 to Interstate 83, which runs into the Airport.

"We got out of New York City by taking the commuter subway, the "tube" I believe it's called, to Newark where the cars were waiting.

"The bombs were rather simple radio frequency explosive devices. Just meant to frighten the Russian delegates who take their afternoon stroll by those buildings every day. When they were near the devices, we detonated them. At the time that was going on, Juan and I were calling the press and the mainland Chinese delegation."

"Just a minute, Perez."

"Yes, Masters?"

"Why the Chinese communist delegation?"

"That you will understand later. For now, be content to cause no trouble and no harm will come to either of you."

"But, Perez, you still didn't explain why you need Joyce. She

20

can't be that high up in the Cuban government to take this sort of risk."

"You're correct, we do have a specific use for the lady."

Chapter 2
THE LOGIC OF IT

I sat next to Joyce and felt a great deal of uneasiness in my stomach. Many possible plots moved through my head, but none made any sense. Finally I leaned over to Joyce and whispered, hoping she would know the answer. "Do you have any idea why or what they plan? It's obviously not ransom. There has been no talk to indicate money."

"It's sort of a ransom, Steve. If I read between the lines correctly, we're to be used as barter. Fidel has recently jailed several members of El Movimiento Nuevo Politica. I believe they wish to negotiate a swap - me for them."

"Then why the bombs in New York? They could have done the swap without the bombs."

"Yes, but they need to embarrass the Castro regime and show the Russians of the trouble potential. Furthermore, this type of guerilla activity serves to strengthen the resolve of the groups' members. It also makes it easier to recruit new members dissatisfied with the Castro government."

How am I a nice bonus? The Castro government doesn't see me as a valuable tool to swap"

"You are a nice bonus because in an American jail is Jose' Francia, one of the great revolutionary leaders of this group. You could be offered for his return. He was arrested in Miami a year ago. He was running illegal guns and ammunition for the revolutionaries in Cuba when U.S. authorities apprehended him."

"I don't mean to interrupt, but if my history serves me correct, Jose' Francia was a dictator in Paraguay who died in 1840. He was one of the founding fathers that chose to isolate Paraguay and move for independence."

"This Jose' Francia is a great, great whatever grandson to the "El Supremo" of Paraguay! Unfortunately, the relative only shares the vanity and solidarity of the original, not all the other qualities."

"I wasn't aware dictators had over-riding good qualities."

"Don't be so damn smug. Very few people were educated in his country in 1813. Jose' had to write the by-laws the government was to operate under, and be sure all was carried out. He was an honest man interested in the progress of the country and it did prosper under his control. He even cared for the aborigine like the Guarani Indian people.

"Some say the young Jose' has visions of a dictatorial philosophy similar to El Supremo. It certainly explains the desire for insurrection. But this is without the usual opposite political philosophy involved. Here we have two essentially identical groups. Not democracy vs. communism as in other such conflicts in the latin countries."

"You know, we don't have two forms of communism competing in America Joyce. Yet no one can tell the difference between the republican and democratic parties. That faded fifty years ago. In fact, you can't even rely on campaign statements. There really isn't much beyond the overall integrity of the system to keep our politicians in line either. This group is just a vision of things to come. With any luck, we'll be able to talk about it."

"Ladies and gentlemen, the captain has requested that we fasten our seat belts as we are making our approach into Atlanta. On behalf of the captain and crew, we hope that you will stay in your seats and obey

26

all instructions given. We are assured all will be turned free in Atlanta to the authorities. Thank you."

"Leslie forgot to thank us for flying East Coast Airlines. Do you think we could manage to get out in the crowd at Atlanta?"

"No, Steve, they have a man behind us with his weapon in hand."

"OK, I guess we're off to Cuba, unless the security group at Atlanta is able to figure some way to help us, without getting us killed."

"I'm glad we're not in Europe now. There, police tend to storm planes with hijackers. That could be unhealthy for its occupants. They seem to be motioning for you Steve."

"Hey, Masters, up front to the radio. You are to say you and the other passengers are fine and not to attempt to do anything to overtake the plane, because you both are coming with us. We want more fuel in this plane now."

"Hello captain, my name is Stephen Masters. What's been done so far?"

"Well, Mr. Masters, we have informed the tower of altered flight pattern after take-off from Atlanta. Exact destination in Cuba is unknown. And, they are aware of the plane's takeover."

"Good God, look at all those police and heavily armed guards. All Hell will break loose with one false move."

"Here is the radio."

"Hello, this is Stephen Masters and Joyce Hurtado. We are both fine and none of the passengers are harmed. They are going to let the passengers and crew, except for Joyce, myself and the pilot, go free. Please don't do anything. We are going to take an extended trip to --- to somewhere."

"Mr. Masters, this is Atlanta security. We understand your communique. May we speak to Perez Guerra, their leader?"

"This is Perez. What do you want? We told you our demands."

As Perez spoke I watched the look on his face. I couldn't believe the steel-like expression. If there were some coefficient of anger index, I know this man would have surpassed the high point. His sidekick, Juan, was a strange person. Not that being strange is unusual. Hell, one had to be strange to hijack a plane and kidnap people to begin with. But Juan was more than strange. He was like a beast, waiting for the OK to strike. Not a pent-up-motion person, but rather, he had the austere personality of a professional killer.

"You said you want fuel enough to reach Grenada Island. The pilot said you were going to Cuba. That plane is not used for flights of that length. You may not have sufficient range to land."

"Don't you worry where we go. The plane will make it just fine."

"Why do you need Mr. Masters and Ms. Hurtado? We will honor your request for fuel."

"That will be made clear to you after we take off. No more talk. Do what we want. You know what we will do if you try any tricks." Perez handed back the radio apparatus to the pilot and turned to Juan. "Open the doors and get these people off."

"Si, Perez."

"Have two guards at the open door. One at the rear door and one midway on the plane. Juan will stay with the captain. I will watch our special prisoners and be alert on each side of the plane for any actions that indicate an attempt to overtake us."

"Joyce, what is the situation if our governments don't go for the exchange of prisoners? Jose' Francia seems like a dangerous person to set free on society. Plus, the radicals they want set free in Cuba will strengthen the movement there."

"They are a violent group, Steve, not unaccustomed to killing people to accomplish their goals. Let's hope we can escape or the switch can be made. If the opportunity presents itself, we should try to run. Just in case the exchange gets bogged down with international politics and red tape."

The people began to file out of the plane, their faces reflecting the fear they must be feeling inside. I looked out the window towards the terminal building. There were armed swat teams everywhere ready to move in on the plane. I hoped no slipups occurred, or passengers tried to become heroes. All that would be needed to call the swat teams into action would be one shot fired.

"One good note, we took off without incident. I guess I was sort of hoping some miracle would come about whereby we could have been rescued. Fear is something that causes me much anxiety, my whole system is screwed up."

"Aren't we flying a bit low, Perez? What's the purpose? Seems like we could injure a fish if it jumps out of the water too high."

"Don't be stupid, Masters. We are flying low to avoid radar tracking. We are going to land in a remote portion of the island of Cuba."

"Remote - the low plains where sugar is grown is easy to spot a plane by only a few people. Which is all that would be necessary."

"No, Steve, the eastern part of Cuba is mountainous with several ranges that include the Sierra del Cristal, Sierra Nipe, Cuchillas Te Toar, and Sierra de Purial. Elevations group to 4,000 feet. In the southeastern part, the elevations go to 6,000 feet."

"Si, sweet land, and there are many little valleys hidden by the dense tropical foliage. Our people hide in the mountains protected by the dense natural vegetation."

"Are you referring to the caves that honeycomb the mountains?"

"Si, that to Ms. Hurtado. Thanks to the island of Cuba being a limestone platform, all the mountains share these caves to some extent. Some of the caves can hide an army of men and supplies."

"Being an American with little guerilla warfare experience, ..., didn't Castro do the same thing? He isn't a fool, and probably knows the hills well. How long do you think you can hide from him?"

"We have done well so far Mr. Politician. The troops of Castro do look for us, but we are not found. Our supplies of weapons and other essentials grow, as does our following. We wait as the premier spreads himself too thin world-wide on his puppet mission for the Russians."

"I know, you will then strike and take over the island."

"Exactly. We are not seen as a serious threat. Only a nuisance to the government. They are not aware of how powerful the movement has become. Castro grows bolder in his attempts at worldwide political insurrection. The troops left behind are not the prime soldiers. They are more like recruits and reserves.... I must go see the pilot to be sure he understands our directions."

"Joyce, I don't like the sound of this. He's serious. I was joking when I said take over the island. They feel they can do it."

"They could be a real threat to the Cuban government" I whispered back in a panic.

"Not just that, we will see and know where these reserves are kept in the mountains. How can they exchange us?"

"Oh Hell, we could lead authorities to where they house the revolutionary movement. We will be killed once they have a way to free the other prisoners. Do you think we would have a chance at jumping from the plane? It seems we're flying low enough."

"Don't be fooled. We're below radar, but not low enough to jump. Besides, what do we do once we're in the water? The guards are too well armed to make any moves here. Their weapons are crude but effective in this short range."

"Our strategy will be to try and hide in the mountains at the first opportunity once we escape."

"Well, Stephen, it appears we may have our own form of international cooperation borne out of necessity. Si, this could be a hallmark for politics and equality womanhood."

"Don't be cute at a time like this Joyce. Jesus Christ, we are near death and you're talking about equal rights for women." I stared at the water and the ridges of waves raised by my eyes because of the speed of travel. Much like how

telephone poles flip by when
traveling in a car only faster. It
was beginning to give me a headache,
but it kept my mind from being so
intense on the problems at hand.

Chapter 3
THE TRUTH OF IT

The approach for the landing was scary at best. The chosen valley was well hidden in the southeastern range. The plane circled to the southwest around the island of Cuba rather than try and fly overland to reduce the risk of being picked up on radar. The entry was from the Gulf of Manzanillo as far as I could tell.

The flight was long and certainly the route would tax the flight limits of this small size jet. But, I was thankful for its size when the landing area came into view.

Before me lay what looked like a narrow fairway on a golf course. Somewhat reminiscent of the narrow

courses cut into the Pennsylvania
mountains, where the trees overhang
along the fairway and if your shot
isn't perfect, either too high or
wide, it will get caught in the
leaves.

The same theory held true here.
We hoped the pilot could bring the
plane in and keep her low, straight
and short. The runway didn't look
4,000 feet and the ground was low
and covered with shrubs and grass,
not the smooth and friction aiding
hard airport type surface.

The plane touched down. It was
easy to tell the pilot was doing
everything short of dragging his
heels to stop us in time. But, all
things considered, a good landing.

I sat for a couple of minutes trying to clear my head and steady the nerves. My stomach was a bit unsteady, but I wanted to thank the pilot for a tremendous job. Joyce and I opened the door and froze in disbelief. The pilot's throat had been cut with a knife and blood was everywhere. Juan killed him immediately after landing so he couldn't describe how or the location where he flew us. The look in Juan's eyes resembled a real fanatic. His half smile and look of accomplishment at the pilot's dead body gave me a hard lump of fear in my throat. The revolutionary just kept smiling at the body in the pilot's chair. His arms limp at his side with his head laying back with the gaping slit in his throat. I looked at the dead pilot with tears in my eyes. His children and wife, if he had them, would never hear his voice, or see him again. This poor unlucky son-of-a-bitch had no desire to be a part of the proposed new order in Cuba.

I stood for a minute in silent prayer. Joyce looked over at me. The non-verbal cues were easy to follow. The nausea felt earlier from a rough landing and fear for our lives skyrocketed. It was all we could do to hold down the desire to vomit.

We were exiting the plane in disbelief accompanied by some not too polite shoves. We walked about a mile or so in silence. It's really strange...you know, when you were a kid and got sick... you wanted your mother. I wanted my mother. Jesus, there was so much yet to tell her. Like a lot of people she never heard how much she was appreciated. I was scared of the unknown ahead. She always made the unknown seem less frightening.

I retained enough composure to try and figure out where we were in relation to anything. Everything looked the same, heavy vegetation all over.

Just ahead was a cabin we were being taken to to stay. Security was tight around it and these guards had weapons that were more deadly than the crude devices used to take the plane. We didn't have any weapons, and were scared to death. They didn't need the overall protection.

The cabin we were in looked as if it once were a home for a plantation foreman or something. Other buildings were in the area all equally old and in need of repair. Obviously abandoned, but there was no sign of huge arms storage, supplies, or troops, necessary to handle a revolution. They must have been stored inside the mountains a few hundred yards behind the cabins.

Joyce stood at the door then turned, and with a very excited tone in her voice said, "Oh my God, Steve, it's Dante Perez." "Who is he?"

"He is the radical king pin behind this group."

"I thought Jose' Francia was the leader?"

"He is a leader, but not the true revolutionary leader in charge of the violence and terrorism. Perez is well educated in the U.S. colleges, but never graduated. He had his first encounters with social unrest in the late 60's era movement in your country. He was a leader with the SDS, as---the ah---Students for Democratic Society among others."

"Why couldn't we have college educated someone that turned out to be a pacifist? What else do you know about him?"

"He spent some time in the Middle East Yemen, I believe, where he learned more and refined his revolutionary tactics. Also in Africa, and finally back in this hemisphere."

"I'm not that familiar with his reputation."

"That's because he doesn't work in the U.S. or Canada. Most of his current efforts are concentrated in Central and South America. The group is responsible for many acts of terrorism, bombings, wrecks and assassinations. Till those people got arrested in the U.S., they weren't known there. They didn't get arrested for terrorism, but for gun running. They were trying to smuggle to Cuba."

"Here is the man now. I think we're going to hear from him in person. No, I think he's ordered us something to drink the way it sounds. Wait---I think we also are getting some different clothes, more suitable for travel."

"I'll go along with that. A three-piece suit doesn't go well in the tropics, nor does your 'lovely outfit'."

"Don't be cute, mine looks similar to a uniform. It's to keep the stares off my body and onto my thoughts."

"No offense meant to your thoughts, but it's hard to avoid the body."

"I can't believe you, we could die at any time and you have sexual visions of my body."

"Always, it's part of the American way. I would have thought you learned that lesson well at Penn State."

"I did, but hope is present that maturity sets in sooner or later with American men."

A big Cuban guard came in and stared at us talking. His patience must have given out. His first remarks were: "Shut up and change into these clothes. Senor Perez will be along soon to speak with you. When changed, here is some Yerba Mate to drink."

"Is there a men's lounge or is this a communal society?"

"Callarse, mudar de ropa!"

"I take it that means No."

"You take it correct Steve. Don't worry, I won't laugh at your legs. And, I don't think he will be watching you anyway."

49

"Usted tener prisa mudar de ropa!"

"Si companero."

Joyce was correct, they didn't watch me change into the drab outfit. The Latin guards had a half leer watching the beautiful slender politician, nude except for panties. My shirt was soaked with sweat, as were my slacks and jacket. While the humidity is high, fear and anxiety were the probable culprits of this much sweat. Joyce was visibly nervous, but keeping a more blank pallor than I could. Of course, she had to keep a bit of control when unclad in the open and one could sense that with any provocation she could be in deep trouble with sexual advances by the guards.

"OK Steve, how do I look in my poncho and pants?"

"Well, they're not designer jeans, but I like the tight fit. However, my tailor was not as careful. But, it all sort of fits, even these awful shoes. If they let me get my bag, I have a pair of sneakers and a jogging outfit in it."

The guard yelled at us to drink..."Sintarse, la bebida."

"What is all this called?"

"The cup is a calabaza, it's sort of a gourd to drink from."

"Why the stick?"

"It's not a stick but a bombilla. Sort of like a tube to drink the mate from."

"I take it "mate" is the general word for tea. This is called Yerba Mate."

"Just think, we could convert you to a Latin in no time. In a matter of minutes you mastered 3 or 4 words."

Dante Perez came through the door. He was with Juan and another member of his group. Dante looked like a serious field general in khaki pants and shirt. He stared at Joyce as if he knew her and offered a stern smile. "Hello Joyce, it's been a long time since we've talked."

"Yes, it has, I went along with Fidel and you chose another path, we have not spoken since."

The tension between the two was apparent. Later conversations with Joyce would reveal they were both bright students and eager to help their country. Both went to college in America. That's where the split began. Dante didn't accept the new Cubanism and went out on his own; away from the influence of Fidel's philosophy. Still, he was interested in his country. A true patriot although his methods were violent.

"I didn't realize you were close friends. My name is Stephen Masters."

"I know who you are. Fortunate for us you were on the plane. It

53

will help us with our plans to return some people from U.S. jails."

"May I mention that my government may not go along with this idea, Mr. Perez."

"Then you will be a sacrifice, a dead sacrifice."

"Uh-huh."

"Dante, it's not Fidel's policy to swap people. You know there is little chance of your plan being a success with me."

"You are important to Fidel, a rising star in the Cuban government. An international symbol of communist equality."

"My God, Joyce, I hope they were paying you well for all this symbolism."

Joyce swung around and whispered in my ear..."Steve, be quiet and stay seated. I don't think your sense of humor is appreciated."

"If Fidel doesn't go along with my plan, you both will be executed and returned home. We have sent our message to both governments and gave them deadlines to reply and how to make the exchange."

"Excuse me, but it's hard to believe you will risk so much just for some prisoners. You could expose much of your operation in this. Why?"

"There are various splinter groups in Cuba. We need a big show here to consolidate them into our movement. And you're correct, we have bigger goals in mind."

"Sounds like a marketing ploy to me."

"Remember, I was educated in the U.S. Some of my courses were marketing. I am not just an idealist, there are certain realities present if we are to achieve our goals. They involve needing a united front. When the time is ripe to strike against Fidel, we will need total support from the other groups to achieve our objectives."

"Yes, but aren't you just substituting Fidel with another communist group that is similar? If my understanding is correct, some of the groups you need support from are allied with U.S. objectives."

"We are not capitalists, that is true, or are we puppets to Russia bleeding Cuba of her strength. We wish to bring our Latin neighbors into a united front of our own. Apart from Russian and U.S. interest. Neither of them give a damn about our people, only their own selfish interests."

"That must involve some support from mainland China. How can they be different?"

"It is different. They don't desire to dictate our policy, just help to achieve the goal of united political philosophy across Latin America. They have been active in that regard for some time."

"I am aware of limited involvement."

"Yes, it's limited, but not as limited as you believe. Much of the support for the guerilla action in Venezuela, Chile and Brazil comes from China. Their support is spread over many groups."

"Why so many groups?" I asked. Dante seemed eager to answer. From his perspective, it was sort of like probabilities and statistics risk spreading, or in the common vernacular - not putting all their eggs in one basket. Some of these groups will be successful. By spreading the support over many groups in each country, they are bound to hit a winner.

"Your president is a hot head. He will react quickly with some form of military action. The most logical one is a blockade. Especially when it is discovered another attack is being launched. Only this one is an information leak designed to insure the blockade.

"This plan will embarrass Fidel and cause great problems with the Russians who will not step in that far away. There will be a lot of accusations between the two super powers.

"The time will be ripe for us to move against Fidel with what appears to be a popular uprising and a plea not to let outside armies enter. The U.S. blockade will make exiles out of Fidel's troops. The task will still not be easy, but more manageable." Dante smiled and leaned forward, indicating there was even more to help his plan. "What will also help is the Chinese backed guerillas will be sure Fidel's troops are kept busy fighting for their own lives wherever possible. China's premier has also assured us that they will send enough verbal blasts to both super powers to keep the situation in as much confusion as possible."

"We are moving you both in two days. I suggest you don't try and leave the building. The guard is told to shoot."

"Isn't that a bit "flip" with your exchange hostages?"

"My good fellow, after we make the video tapes...you are dispensable. I would be nice to me if I were you. So senor, the trip is hard across the jungle-like mountains, I suggest you rest."

"Joyce, I think I want to get sick. His plan sounds like it has a remote chance to work. At least part of it. The first part to embarrass the U.S. could work. My God, if he has these people as captives already, it could work."

"Steve, we could die soon. Let's work out how to get out of here. I want to live a little longer. And I want to stop this."

"What sort of action are you planning that will produce the "ripe" time to move against Fidel?"

"Fidel is deploying large numbers of men and arms in Africa, and more are planned. In addition, large numbers are being sent to help guerillas against U.S. backed governments in Central America."

Dante's eyes were afire with excitement and he leaned forward to speak. "What is needed is a reason for the U.S. to take action; either by aid to these countries or by another blockade of Cuba. The blockade will have the effect of preventing the return of troops or Russian help.'

"What could possibly do that?" I asked looking a bit inquisitive.

Dante began to strut and smile, sort of like the cat that ate the canary look, then spoke. "A two part objective. First, major incident in Cuba, made to look like a CIA backed mission. Everyone knows the financial woes of Cuba. Any serious setback more than already suffered would cause chaos. The sugar refineries and storage cooperatives are prime targets for this."

After he dropped this bomb shell, he stood quiet and watched for expression on our faces. His objectives sounded like a "pipe dream" to achieve. It would require luck, timing and realistic plans.

Cuba was in trouble, the five year plans weren't working, the agriculture program was crucial for Fidel. I looked up at Dante and stared at him. He began to speak again. "Within the next few days the sugar plant will be destroyed."

"How can you possibly hit all of them?"

"Joyce, don't be a fool" he said, "We need hit only the major one, around Mat Anzas, the western part, or the two largest inland refineries. That will cause the turmoil necessary to create accusations, especially when CIA men are found dead at the scene."'

I smiled. There seemed to be a crack in the plan already, "The U.S. government, I can assure you, will not send volunteers, my limited exposure as a public official in Pennsylvania is safe to go on for that."

"We have our volunteers. The CIA foolishly sent persons here to meet with U.S. allied groups. We were able to, how you say, recruit them. They are in prison in a cave in the western region of the country in the Sierra del Rosario. These little hills have many fine caves with the beautiful stalactites and stalagmites and whatever else is part of limestone caverns, near to the scene for easy transport, and virtually impossible to find their location till we are ready."

"Dante, how will this cause the U.S. to go into action?"

"It won't Joyce, but it will bring the other groups around to supporting the El Movemiento Nuevo Political. Remember there is a two part plan. The second will bring the U.S. into action, the incident to spring a U.S. boycott will come from an incident

In Miami. Within a week the five day U.S.-Pan American conference will be held in Miami at the research center on Key Biscayne across from the Sea Aquarium."

"I know where that is located. It's not a political conference, but one concerning fish, and killer bees and that sort of stuff. That's the kind of center it is

"Senor, there will be many U.S. State Representatives present. We are going to blow up the center and leave certain evidence there."

"What type evidence, Dante?"

"Joyce, I am almost sorry to say this, but we will have a major in Fidel's personal guard present. He has sympathy to our goals. Only he doesn't know he is to die in this encounter. Plus, there will also be found two Russian military advisors. They are well hidden along with the CIA persons within the caves in the mountains. It will appear like a quick hitting guerilla attack in retaliation for the bombing of the sugar industry in Cuba."

Chapter 4
BEHIND IT ALL

Practically every. T.V. station in Pennsylvania was carrying the Governor's message live. A plea from the governor and the people of the state for the safe return of the Secretary of Labor, and the Cuban attaché was made.

There were newsbreaks by the major networks nationwide that delivered the message of the terrorists. A swap of prisoners or the young politician dies. More information about Stephen Masters, Secretary of Labor for the State of Pennsylvania, was given publicly than even he would have cared to hear.

In addition to the T.V. announcement, the Governor was in

contact with the President to try and see what could be accomplished through official channels as quickly as possible. But the news from Washington was always grim. The messages were only one way, from them to us. No way to start any dialogue or hurry the matter.

The Cuban government was embarrassed to admit they did not Know where the hostages were being held. Only deep concern for both members of the party.

Outside of a rather well-known and long established restaurant in the Georgetown district of Washington, Robert Jamison, Chief of Strategy for the State Department's private "research" council was exiting a cab.

The site at the corner of Wisconsin and "M" streets housed the group. It's front, and for all obvious speculation, is what it appears to be; a popular restaurant-bar. The food is excellent; French-Italian cuisine. The bar is staffed with bartenders who not only mix a generous drink, but a very good drink. All combine to provide a level of traffic to mask the comings and goings of the group.

Beyond the restaurant, the rest of the building is devoted to the private research council of the State Department. Research in the title is used to coincide with the special talents of the persons recruited to work for the council. All are professors, Ph.D.'s, politicians or in some way well educated and technically trained persons who can be reasonably passed off as research people. The reality of the group is an elite undercover body for the State Department.

Robert Jamison enters through the bar and walks into the toilet and presses his hand on the tiny mirror. A reading is taken of the print and matches a file of prints. The door opens to what appears to be a storage closet in the bathroom. Passing through the closet is another door. This one with a series of numbered buttons that resemble a push button phone. With the proper sequence entered, Jamison enters the general reception area and walks to the main strategy conference room.

It's only one hour since the terrorists sent their message. The others of the strategy group have met since the hijacking was first known. They awaited Jamison's input to any decisions that need be made.

Jamison is one of those unknown to the general public persons who operate in the Washington power network. In regular touch with cabinet officials, senators, congressmen, pentagon high-up's, and the President, but never photographed or mentioned.

America may lack for consistent foreign policy, but Jamison and his crowd have been there since Eisenhower's days. Ike was not especially good at some aspects of foreign policy, and the group began as a way to rectify problems caused by Ike or to serve as another way to help fight the cold war.

Jamison has always kept their mission on target. Unlike the CIA, whose activities are very broad ranged and may include almost anything. The "Research" unit confines itself to sensitive diplomatic problems.

The council makeup includes former cabinet occupants of the Secretary of State and Defense advisors to the President, Generals and high-ups in the CIA and FBI. The CIA and FBI members to the strategy serve as a sort of double agent within the secret agencies loyal to the U.S. government. In addition, there are members affiliated with the research unit world-wide who provide a network of special information essential for remedial foreign policies.

"Sorry I'm late, but I was held up by some rather disturbing information I will pass on to you later. However, our immediate concern is for our agent. The political exposure of our agent makes for certain risks, but the probability of this happening is rare."

"Robert, it's my opinion that we assume our agent is dead and plan a replacement."

"The CIA has numerous replacements, our tedious recruitment process and long training makes it very difficult to secure agents, let alone one placed in a unique position such as this. But you're correct in one respect. Both hostages may be killed rather than let free if the exchange is made."

"Our information in the Defense Department shows various reports on these splinter groups and the arms buildup. But this sort of action has not been in their plans before.

The Secretary of Defense leaned back in his chair and stared at Robert and then at the Assistant to Robert Jamison who was about to speak. "Excuse me, but Robert, didn't we help the FBI to capture this Jose' Francia they want released?"

"Yes, we wanted to avoid just a change of shirts of leadership if Cuba does have a revolution. Besides arms buildup. Francia was bringing in these Guarani Indians from

Paraguay and eastern Bolivia. They're not much above primitive Bushmen, but are fierce in fighting. Their hope was to have a sort of death squad made up of this group. His capture stopped not only guns but the continued import to Cuba of these Guarani.

"Let me recount to you some rather disturbing news I've been given and let's see if it's connected to this activity. It appears that Chinese-backed guerilla movements in South and Central America are massing in larger numbers near the position of the Cuban-backed guerilla troops."

"Mr. Jamison, maybe Castro has altered his allegiance to Russia as some have suggested."

"There's another thought gentlemen. At the interrogation of Jose', he did mention that there was support for their movement even outside of Cuba. Could it be that these groups are the support outside of Cuba?"

"What of the plane and its location?"

"There's been no word on the pilot or plane. We were hoping to find out from him where they may be located. We can assume he has been executed."

"Robert."

"Yes, Admiral,"

"In our discussions before you arrived we had tossed about the mission of our agent in Miami, beyond the obvious public one.

Wasn't it to find out why the activity in Cuba and its unusual course of events?"

"You're correct. This is certainly a strange beginning to a counter revolution, but go on."

John Greyson from the CIA stood up, brandy in hand and began to speak. "Well, as it appears, there are certain points that crop up. We can't refer to them as facts because there isn't enough information to make such a strong statement. First, we've not heard backed revolutionaries. There's no word either from our agent or any official message from Habana that they were captured, which tends to make one believe another revolutionary group has captured them. Second, the activity of this group in procuring arms. Some of the arms recovered were stored for apparent use in the Miami area; not for transit to Cuba. Third, your new information about the Indians from South America. This doesn't fit with a popular movement uprising. A death squad indicates some special mission or missions."

As the CIA Assistant Director finished, several of the group belted down the remainder of their drinks and headed for refills. Others began to talk among themselves.

"May I say something Robert?"

"Certainly Admiral."

"So far the evidence appears to indicate some form of activity in Cuba and the U.S. In one respect, it's fortunate our agent has been captured. If the person remains alive, we may be able to make the connection and know what we're dealing with here."

"I agree Admiral. We must get down to business and contact our agent's world-wide for information and process a new plan. We don't want to sit back and see. If some incident is being planned that can be stopped, we must be prepared to move."

Chapter 5
FLEE FROM IT

"You know, it's quite cordial of them to provide us with some wine to wash down this, whatever we're eating."

"It's not being nice, it's probably the only liquid fit to drink beside mate. They don't need sick hostages yet."

"Well, if not cordial, it provides a pleasant atmosphere for us."

"Men are all alike, simple functioning at low level biological urges."

"I don't know about all men, but having this lovely lady curled up beside me sharing a blanket is nice."

We sat talking on the blanket for what seemed like moments, yet the hours passed by. It served as a way to calm us both down. Joyce spoke of her early years in Cuba and how so much had changed with the Castro government. Yet, for all his faults, she believed he helped the mass of Cubans live with more self-respect.

I explained my youth and how much I traveled before moving to Pennsylvania as a young school boy. I loved the mountains and change of seasons there. Nothing is more beautiful than the sight Of a stand of hickory trees turned to a beautiful shade of bright yellow in the fall.

We both compared notes on college and the crazy things that

happened or we were involved in. The talking kept our minds off the terror of the moment. The two jugs of wine they left were down to less than half a glass in one.

Considering we were both scared to death, feeling certain that we were to die before being set free, there became an intensity of the moment. I began stroking her hair and cheek. How soft both. were. Reading an unwritten message, T. leaned over and we began to kiss. The embrace and contact of the lips was powerful and aggressive on both our parts. Almost as if it were the last forms of pleasure and reassurance we each would know. Without me saying, but yet thinking it, she said "The guards are not going to bother us. They are in the middle of the opening in front of the cabin. I heard them speak. They think we're already asleep. Besides, there is no way out except past them."

Almost as if it were a religious experience, we undressed each other in a most seductive and touching manner.

Her body shown in the night from the doorway screen. The clothes still revealed beauty while dressed, but undressed, she was Even more than my dream experience.

Foreplay wouldn't have been a necessity, we were both already excited. It was beautiful to touch and kiss her entire body. I was gently kissing her breast and massaging her very firm buttocks when she decided it was time to make love.

I had this immediate fear in the back of my head that the high level of excitement might make this a short-lived encounter of lovemaking. I tried to explain this. She told me to relax. She knew just how to command my moves and hers. She was on top and set the pace until I could regain my composure from having her. We then moved through several positions till we climaxed.

We settled down to sleep, both still nude and very relaxed. Rest would come quickly and easily and it would be needed.

In the next morning's first light we dressed quickly. The guards came in and brought water to wash

with and some of their country tea
to drink.

Dante Perez followed by Juan and
another member of his group came in
and asked if we enjoyed our rest. It
was difficult not to appear both
relaxed and frightened at the same
time. But, Dante had a strange look
on his face and it was easy to tell
he was mad at Juan. Dante was trying
to control his emotions he knew it
was stupid to have killed the pilot
of the plane. He had uses, he was a
trained asset as a pilot. The
message to Guerra was clear. He is
your side-kick, keep him under
control. He ushered his small
contingent outside, he felt the need
to clarify some key issues with
them. He told Joyce he would be
right back.

Dante began to explain again the nature of their complex plan. It was critical that his relatively small group stayed both disciplined and focused. What he learned in the US during the turbulent 1960's was that in order to grow a "movement" they must appear to everyone else that they were in control. To be absolutely certain of their vision and the positive chances of its success. In the US during those years this produced a confederation of radical groups which became very effective and could leverage its numbers far more than anyone of the smaller groups each acting independently. It took constant communications and negotiations. It took appeasement of the various group leaders by Jose' Francia. A reason why Jose' was such a key figure to get exchanged for Joyce. Dante grimaced, though loyal he had his own doubts as well. A lot of pieces had to fall exactly perfect at the needed time for all this to work. Not only to get Francia released, but back in Cuba with them as well. Castro may or may not goa all out to get Joyce back. But he sure as hell did not want a free Jose Francia loose in his country. The notion of this exchange for him was a real long shot. The US rarely ever negotiated with terrorist. Especially for a revolutionary from a communist country. But the idea that Francia could disrupt Castro was the true lure for the US State Department politicos to go along with the exchange.

Dante spoke slowly and clearly to his gathered group. "I know we have threatened to kill them to their faces. And, maybe we will. But not now. Negotiations with all the parties will take time. Despite out threats to both groups-they know better, Remember my friends, it is not like we can just sit across from them and work out the details". "Everything goes through intermediaries". "Do not forget that we must always keep on moving this process forward. And, we must keep moving physically as well to keep from being found." Dante paused for effect before continuing. "If someone loses control and kills them that person will pay with their life!" The silence was amazing, the only sound to be heard was insects and a few bird calls.

Another member of the group spoke up. "I believe the movement of the prisoners will be a real plus with the other revolutionary groups aligned with us". A real motivation for them that we have a good plan- and they can see the negotiation process is still ongoing".

Dante smiled appreciating the positive comment from the member. "You are right- this will work to our advantage." The other groups get to share in the work of guarding the prisoners and strengthen their resolve for the alignment of all of us to overthrow Castro". "Thank you my friends-I must now return to speak with the prisoners." Dante turned and walked toward their cabin. It will be a balancing act. The American would not be too difficult-but Joyce was not only smart but the Castro regime itself was born of revolutionary roots and she could sense any weaknesses.

Steve looked up as Dante came back in and answered his question posed to them before he left, "yes, we rested as well as one can in such conditions. Have you scheduled our release yet, or are we to remain here? Wherever here is?" I looked at Joyce trying to formulate all that has happened in my mind. My own life was not without intrigue, but it could not be left to show Dante and his men. I had to continue to appear to be an almost "clueless" low-level state politician. Certainly I had my misgivings. I had never been captured like this before where the captors seemed somewhat savage in nature. An energy of pent up emotion and on the brink of exploding violence. I was wondering what my real boss and his strategy group were doing to counter all this. They could not give in too quickly or I would not have any chance to get the whole story of what is potentially happening here in the mountains of Cuba. With all this-Joyce could not know all about me as well. Despite being captured with me she was still a loyal Castro appointee. I did not need the sum total of my identity being made public via a Cuban connection.

"Both governments have been notified. We will be in touch with them again today. We need to make a recording of you both to show all is OK. It is a video tape with sound."

"I don't believe I'm dressed for a film debut."

"Masters, you cut the cute remarks or we'll give you the respect your parents failed to teach you."

"He's as scared as I am, Dante. Don't beat up a politician. Their only defense is to shoot off their mouths."

"Okay, follow me."

"Don't stare at me like that. If I didn't step in, your remarks would have cost you some teeth. Your ego will recover, if we live."

As we walked to tape this message, I decided that when this was all over, assuming we would be alive, I was going to take assertiveness training to learn to handle modern women. I was raised in a rural Pennsylvania town with rural values. Even the preacher told us to be gentlemen. Maybe it was because my mother was too forceful during toilet training. Hell, all I know is that I keep ending up in sexual encounters where I jump to the tune of my domineering partner.

By the time we reached the cabin, my ego began to recover. felt a lot for Joyce. Besides, all things said it was nice to get laid before I die.

"Sit down together, read this message to your governments and don't do anything stupid. This isn't live T.V., but a video cassette. We will erase what we don't like."

The message said we were alive
and well and that our location was
impossible to trace. Please
cooperate and we would be alive. The
only trouble with their plan was
that it called for a two stage
release of prisoners. With us being
the second stage. It made us suspect
that we may not receive the type of
respect desired once the first stage
release of prisoners from Cuba and
the U.S. was accomplished.

We were allowed to walk around
for a short period once the tape was
filmed. A guard was following us
with enough fire power to convince
us not to try and run for it. The
courier with the tape took off
toward the air landing strip where a
small engine plane would pick up the
film and the courier. The process of

delivery involved several steps so as not to give a direct link to where we were hiding.

Joyce and I made mental maps of every tree, bush, building, and path we could walk near or see. When not making love or talking the night before, we were carefully noting guard schedules and movements. We figured that at dusk we should begin to try some form of escape. The idea of waiting to be recovered by a rescue team or by prisoner exchange didn't come off as a good gamble.

I realized I was scared, hungry, and a bit tired, but I couldn't believe one thing. Watching Joyce, walk about in her revolutionary outfit was erotic. It must be the psychological aspect of being thrust together under conditions that could result in our death at any time. But had it not been for the guard, who I was convinced also had his share of fantasies, I would have been tempted to act out my fantasy. I whispered to Joyce of my feelings at the moment. Coming from the Aquarian age of expressing one's true feelings, it was not so amazing a thing to do. Unfortunately, she thought me a lunatic and couldn't imagine how one could feel that way in the middle of a jungle prison camp in daylight, with guards watching us with machine guns. I was told in no uncertain terms to think of an escape plan and concentrate on the topography, not her. Erotic fulfillment would be after we got out of here. What role reversal. I'm a romantic and she's a pragmatic realist!

It was dusk. We had eaten, if one calls wine and stale bread a meal. But this wasn't the Hilton. The guards wouldn't be back for an hour, and that would be the last real check for the night. We began to work loose the tile in the cottage we were.in. The cottage - house, whatever, was built up off the ground about two feet with a crawl space underneath.

From the mental notes of the area, we could, in theory, crawl under the house to a bougainvillea hedge, probably dating back to the plantation days judging from the size, and move along the outer edge of it to some trees. There it got tricky. The next move was to the edge of the forest area. But, it was a plan - however difficult and negatively lopsided in the probabilities of success.

The first step was to remove the red spanish tile floor from over the timber floor. Tearing up some tile was not hard, only tedious. Some were already loose, and the grout that hold the tile in place isn't like real concrete. Besides, these were light enough to be laid over the timber floor.

Thanks to some industrious termites, the boards were not as serious a problem as we first feared.

Both of us began the process by scratching like wild nervous kids at the floor till we calmed down enough to be systematic. I used my belt buckle to pry at the tile and grout while Joyce started to dig at the wood with her nails and belt buckle. Even though we were making progress, the sweat was running down our hands as if someone was dripping water from a glass. The humidity was high in the tropics, but this was all nerves. We wanted to shout with excitement when the first board was ripped up. The process continued for a few more boards by banging and picking as quietly as possible.

Before our leaving the cabin, we had to be in our proper sleeping positions near the door in clear view to pass bed check. It was about time for the guard to come around.

As we lay there, the guard came and stared in the door at us. Then the unexpected, he hit the door with his hand to enter. Joyce jumped to an upright position to ask what was wrong. The guard made a suggestive remark about her body. She told him that Dante had claimed the first rights and he could take the matter up with him because he hadn't succeeded yet. The guard slammed the door and left.

"Thank goodness you think fast. Another few feet in here and he would have spotted the loose tiles and boards in back. That would have meant we take him out, which would have given us about 20 minutes until we would have been checked on."

We lost no time in pulling up the rest of the boards to make our descent to the crawl space. We couldn't replace the boards above us and hoped they would check elsewhere before looking and figuring out our route.

The crawl space had termite mounds and filth to crawl through. Being a gentleman, I went first. The bugs crawled over our hands and spider webs were in our face and hair. I hoped none of the spiders who became displaced were mad enough to bite.

Behind me, Joyce was doing battle with a scared rat. I turned and started swinging at it with a stick, trying to persuade it that we were more uncomfortable and scared than it was. Palmetto bugs, I guess, were running for life. They looked like the ones in Miami. God, they felt horrible when they squirmed out from under your hands. I finally caught the rat with a good smack and

knocked it out or killed it. I
didn't care. It didn't move and I
wasn't interested enough to go
check.

We got to the end of the house
and started for the bougain-villea
hedge. I looked back and saw what
looked like a snake. For all I know,
it could have been an old piece of
hose. But it scared the hell out of
me, and made me leap into the hedge.
Bougainvillea is a plant with large
thorns and is very effective as a
protective hedge. It was all I could
do to keep from crying in pain from
the thorns.

We weren't fifty feet from where
we made our start and I was already
in pain, uncomfortable from dirt,
bugs, rats, and wondering if this
was the correct idea.

Joyce led the scramble down the hedge row. At the end, we darted from tree to bush till we got to the forest, where we both bolted behind some vegetation. I let out a yelp. Not too loud. I was out of breath. There in front of me was a four foot lizard on the limb of a tree. I thought it was a carryover from the dinosaur era and saw me as its next lunch. Frozen, I stared. Joyce cupped her hand over my mouth and threw a stick at it and the damn thing left.

"Haven't you ever seen an iguana before in Miami? They're harmless."

"Not up close, four feet long, when I am scared to death-"

"There are no dangerous snakes or other animals in Cuba. The only one that is a bit troublesome is the Boa, but we won't have any problems with them. Now, shut up and let's move."

"If memory serves me correct, the vehicles should be down this way." Pointing to a well-trodden path about 100 yards from the cottage where we were held.

"I believe you're correct. But don't just wander down the middle. Damn politicians have no sense of what is going on around them."

"That was an uncalled for remark, I'm tired, have bug bites, spiders in my hair and wondering if this is all worth it. So where do we go if not on the path?"

"Follow me, if your ego will allow. I followed you out of the house into a rat and saw you fall into a thorn hedge, Maybe I can do better."

"Why couldn't you have been a quiet Japanese diplomat with respect for men?"

We paralled the path with greater ease than I thought, and, as would be expected, Joyce was correct. A guard was walking the path to the vehicles.

"You have to take him out! Can you do that?"

"You know I've never knocked anyone on the head to 'take them out' in my life. It's not one of the job requirements to be a politician. All we do is pull the wool over people's eyes."

"What?"

"Don't worry, I'll do it. Let me find a club."

As we approached the parking area of the vehicles, the guardstood talking to another guard. Joyce said they were changing shifts. I bolted from the brush across about ten feet of clearing and crouched behind a jeep. I did that without conferring with. Joyce. And by the look on her face, it was a stupid move. But, I had a plan. I remembered a T.V. show where Hutch crawled around a car and under another to surprise a guy. Joyce obviously didn't have my frame of reference and depth of data from T.V., shows to draw upon.

The other guard headed back the path toward the cottages. I waited a few moments and began carefully moving around the jeep to position

myself beside a truck next to the
jeep.

In all, there were five vehicles
in this row and three in the next.
The opening was about 150 feet
across and 100 feet wide with a road
at the one end in the middle of the
far side and it exited at the bottom
of the opening at the other and
formed a loop.

The guard was in front of the
truck at the right fender. It was
the first of the five vehicles on
that row. As I crawled under the
truck and began to move, the
unexpected happened. He began to
walk away toward the jeep where I
had been. Christ, didn't he realize
I didn't plan on him moving? Sweat
was pouring down my body. The dirt
was caking on my face and hands. I

had to think of a different plan. My next move was to position myself where I could see him. By the time I carefully moved to that position so as not to attract attention, he moved again. This was beginning to resemble a Three Stooges movie.

This movement took him to the edge of the clearing near Joyce. My heart was in my throat. I was positioning myself to leap out and save her at any cost. I couldn't believe my eyes. She stood up and kicked him in the groin, a shot I could hear and almost feel. Then she took the stick in her hand and placed a home run type hit on his head while he was bending over holding what remained of his manhood. All with such speed I barely could get out from under the truck before the poor guy was out.

"Holy crap, Joyce, it was my duty to take him out. You could have been killed. Is he okay?"

"Waiting for you to quit playing musical cars could take all night. Let's find one with keys and sabotage the others. Here, the Fiat has keys in it."

"Flip to see if it has any gas. I will start with the three trucks, then the jeeps to make sure they can't be used to get us."

I opened the hood and yanked a wire or two and hoped that would keep them out of service.

We heard a guard call out while walking down the path. When his shift ended on the watch, he went to get a drink for his friend and was now returning. I grabbed the tire iron from the front jeep and crouched beside a bush to wait for him. The other guard we had dragged off to the side was not easily visible so as to provide a warning of trouble. When he approached, I hit him on the side of the head and headed for the Fiat. My only pause was to grab his pistol, figuring it might come in handy.

I got in the driver's side and started the engine, shifted into first gear and headed for the road by the closest exit to the parking area. As I swung the car out, the guard I hit with the iron started to move. I couldn't believe it. I had hit him hard. His rifle was picked up and fired. He stood and his knees buckled under him. But that was enough. There would be a swarm of people upon this spot quickly. Our only hope was to dart down the road quickly.

Chapter 6
THE CHASE

Perez Guerra ran down the path with some men to the clearing where the vehicles were kept. The guard attempted to stand, but was still unable.

"Tell me what happened!"

"I was hit, I did not see by who. They took my pistol and the Fiat."

"The 'who' was the prisoners? Go tell Dante what has happened. We will take the jeeps and go after them."

The guard ran back the path and across the compound to where Dante stood and listened with a look on his face that resembled an angry lion.

"The prisoners have escaped with the Fiat. They ambushed the guards. But, I do not know how they got out of the cabin. We were out in the yard area and no one went by us."

"Let's go see how they escaped. Is Perez going after them?"

"Si, Dante."

"Juan, put out the word that I want these people back, alive, if possible. Let the other revolutionary groups know it will be Worth their trouble to help capture them."

"Si."

"Look, they went out through the floor. We checked them and they were asleep. I don't understand. I saw them myself."

"I do", said Dante. He nodded to Juan. Dante walked out the door and started slowly for the path, waiting for Juan.

With lightning speed, Juan slit the throat of the guard as he did with the plane captain. The blood was washing out of his body onto the floor and draining down the hole in the floor where the two captives had escaped. Juan smiled and put the knife back; but only temporarily. The two at the clearing would receive the same greeting.

Stupidity and mistakes of this nature cannot be tolerated. El Movemiento Nuevo Politica couldn't function if staffed by fools. At the clearing, the guard hit by Joyce was still unconscious. A point of mercy considering hi pending fate. His throat was cut where he lay. The other guard saw this and even in a weakened state tried to crawl away. The dirt packed under his fingernails as he attempted to pull away along the ground. His lower body refused to obey the commands of his brain. Juan kicked him in the side. The snapping sound signaled the breaking of several ribs. The guard rolled on his back; the blood began to trickle slowly out of his mouth, but he mustered the energy to speak. "I beg you I did not see them. I had no way to know they were there. I was only bringing a drink back. Please, have I not been loyal and worked hard for the cause of the movement?"

Dante was about to give in on this case when a sudden movement by one of the female soldiers occurred before he could speak.

She was the girlfriend of the guard on the ground and carried a machete. Instead of defending or arguing for his life, she looked at him on the ground, spit on him, called him a fool who could ruin the movement, and with a flip of both hands brought the machete down on the man's neck, almost cutting off his neck. Juan smiled at the girl. Dante started to get sick at the mess of blood from the two bodies and walked away.

The other guards gathered up the bodies to bury in a ditch nearby. The graves would be unmarked so as not to draw attention to the camp by Fidel's troops who are always on patrol for revolutionaries. The tropical vegetation would cover the spots quickly. No signs would remain of this incident.

The road was nothing but a wagon path, barely wide enough for one vehicle. Probably only a dirt road cut out of the woods to service the former estate,. The holes in the road were not filled and the tire ruts were deep, causing the Fiat to bottom out in many spots.

"They are gaining on us. I can see their lights coming. Can't this car go any faster?"

"I'm going as fast as possible on this road. I'll never again complain about Penn Dot highway maintenance if this ordeal ends safely."

The turns were sharp and the clutch was in need of repair. This made downshifting a real trick. We started up an incline. The car was agile, but underpowered. This is where they will close the gap.

A bullet shattered the back window and lodged too close for comfort. Joyce leaned out the window and fired a shot into their windshield. This slowed them a bit till we hit the top of the hill. On the down side, I threw the car wide open in the straights and was downshifting in the turns by double clutching,

The jeep tried to pull up next to us on the left. I hit into an S turn to the right and downshifted into the left part of the turn. As is customary with those vehicles, the speed and angle of the turn was too sharp and the jeep rolled over, coming to rest against a tree. The other jeep was a little further back and easing through the turns. Perez was in that vehicle.

We made it around the series of turns and I noticed further down the road an even smaller path off to the right. The road bed on the right had a ramp-like lip and was bordered by thick brush.

"Let's give them something to think about, Joyce."

"Which road are you going to take, Steve?"

"Neither. We are going over the edge and hiding."

"Do you know what you're doing?"

"I hope so."

At that point, I killed the lights and went up over the lip of the road. The car felt like it went airborne for a few feet and settled behind some bushes. There I eased her up a bit to remain hidden and shut off the engine.

"Are you okay, Joyce?"

"Yes, just a lump on my head from the flight and sudden landing."

Joyce pulled up the pistol she took from the first guard and I pulled out the one from the guard I hit. I still wondered if the poor guy she kicked would ever speak in a normal voice again.

Perez's jeep raced by where we were hiding. We could see him motion to the right fork in the road. We watched as he went down the road and around a turn.

I quickly started up the Fiat and proceeded carefully to drive out of the mess I flew us into. I jumped out and Joyce shot behind the driver's seat. The damn car was lodged on the pile of leaves and soft dirt. I pushed the little car till it was on the road and jumped into the passenger side figuring we had lost our pursuers and all was okay now.

Joyce shot down the left fork, which is the actual road we were on. We went around the first turn and approached the second. We were about to turn the lights on when around the second turn our stomachs and hearts went into our mouths. We couldn't believe our eyes. There was Perez's jeep only in front of us.

The right fork was only a loop that reconnects back to the main road.

The surprise was more than they could handle also. The momentary lack of strategy on their part was enough for Joyce. She downshifted the Fiat and passed them on the last of the second turn. I opened fire and laced the jeep with bullets. It worked; we were around them. But, I only had a shot left, and Joyce had three or four. We were coming down the mountain into what appeared to be an area of rolling countryside where we would quickly be caught. We had to do something to force the jeep to go off the road and end its presence.

I yelled to Joyce to pull the emergency brake with all her might with her one hand and turn the wheel as far left as possible and floor the gas pedal of the car while doing so.

She performed the maneuver beautifully. The car, as we anticipated, made a perfect close U-turn. The ass end swung around with the tires and brakes smoking. The car lurched forward with the transmission rattling and the pistons pounding their little hearts out.

Perez's driver was caught off guard by the sudden change in direction of our car, and tried to spin around to follow our maneuver. The jeep strained on the gravel and dirt. But, the force of inertia was

too great for the awkward vehicle
and it gave way and rolled over.
Bodies flew out everywhere.

Joyce repeated the maneuver to
head out of the mountain. The last
thing we wanted to do was head back
to the camp. As we went by, I placed
a shot and hit one of the men who
was heading for us from the side. I
then threw the pistol at another who
was lying on the road unconscious.

We pushed the Fiat for all it
was worth to get out of the
mountains and raced across the open
country. Not slowing there for fear
of more pursuers to follow. I
expressed my amazement that she was
able to handle those maneuvers with
the car so well. As it turned out,
she had been to one of those driving
schools that teach diplomats,

corporate executives, their drivers, and the like, how to perform such actions. With all the political kidnapping, such knowledge is sometimes necessary.

She was more amazed that I was so well versed behind the wheel of a car. A foreign car at that. "All I own are foreign cars. An American made car would have fallen apart trying an escape on that road. Besides, the main reason is, I don't like seeing myself coming and going. If you buy a Mustang, Camaro, or Firebird, you don't have a special car. They make around 15,000 of each per week. In a few months, that's more than the historic run of MG or Fiat Spider. Plus, you never know what you're getting. In an MG or Fiat, everything is standard. In

American cars, everything is an option. From suspensions to paint. Hell, there is no standardization."

"Steve, enough about cars. It will be dawn soon. Do we drive during the daylight? And where do we drive to?"

"Joyce, relax, you're safe here. This is your country. Can't we simply go over to an army officer or police and get help? We must stop their plan to attack the sugar refinery and make it look like an international incident."

We raced across the open road to a small village ahead, hoping we could find some police to help us. Fatigue was beginning to take its toll on both of us. I had the window open and rubbed spit on my eyelids to stay awake. I knew everything would be OK and the police or army would help us. The sense of relief didn't help me stay awake."

"Isn't that an army jeep ahead? Let's stop them and get help."

"You just sit and look important Steve. I'll talk to them."

Joyce hopped out of the jeep and began to tell them who we were and what we wanted. A peculiar thing began to happen - there were two soldiers in the jeep and one opened a manila folder and acted as if he were comparing a picture to the person and showed the other soldier. They began asking her why she became a traitor to the cause of Fidel and helped the rebels.

Joyce looked stunned. She turned and said they thought we were traitors. I didn't waste a moment. The soldiers had to be taken out before they could get their guns or call for help.

It always amazes me what fear can do to a fatigued body. shot up like I just had eight hours sleep. I picked up the pistol of Joyce's from the seat and screamed. The soldiers looked and Joyce told them to put up their arms. I didn't know enough Spanish or the Cuban version of Spanish to say it so my scream had to do. The Spanish in Cuba is so mixed liberally with African words brought over from the slavery era. My three years of Spanish in secondary school was fairly useless.

We took their pistols and the spare gas with us. The guards were tied and driven in their jeep behind some bushes where they wouldn't be found for some time.

We headed down the road further to get away and to try and figure out what just happened. There was a wind break of sorts ahead between two fields. We decided to go into it and sleep while it was light and to make some plans. It was a whole new situation confronting us. The folder the soldiers had indicated that Joyce was a rebel sympathizer and myself a CIA infiltrator. This was released by the kidnappers in Cuba and the U.S. The swap was to the U.S. for both of us. Locally, in Cuba, we were to be used to generate support for the rebel movement by

Joyce's conversion and my capture. Perez fooled us both, and was master. The death of Joyce would be blamed on authorities and my death would be a credit to the movement. A win-win scenario, for them, till we left. We had to get out of Cuba. But not before we tried to stop the plot in the eastern range.

The sleep would feel good, however little we may allow ourselves. The car was hidden and we nestled under some bushes to rest. Ordinarily, the thought of such a spot would not seem comfortable. Exhaustion made the cluster of trees and bushes resemble a fancy hotel.

Chapter 7
THE OTHER FRONTS

Arthur Harrington sat in the damp cool cave in the narrow Sierra del Rosario Mountains. He couldn't believe he was this close to Habana and the authorities didn't know of its location. If they did find him, he would be tried as a spy and imprisoned. The CIA was not a popular group in Cuba. Especially since the Bay of Pigs fiasco.

Most rebel groups are filled with spies and turncoats. They either lose conviction to the cause or find that betrayal has great monetary rewards. Even the Castro movement was riddled with those who were working for Batista. This group didn't appear to have that problem or a location this close to Habana could not survive.

As in the case of Castro, the main base of operations is the eastern part of the country. The revolution for Castro began in the Sierra Maestro. Control was fairly assured after the strategic city of Santa Clara fell on December 31, 1958. Batista left on New Year's Day.

From the first steps of Columbus on this island on his maiden voyage October 28, 1492, the island of Cuba has had a history of Fighting, revolutions, and control of her people not by popular choice. The British took the island from Spain in 1762, gave it back, and then took it again. Later, it went back to Spain. In the 1820's, the U.S.,

France and Great Britain all wanted to take control from the cruel and autocratic Spanish domination.

At one point in 1848 there was talk of annexation of Cuba to the U.S. and many subversive plots were organized, all unsuccessful. Arthur laughed to himself. He liked the island and her people. He vacationed here in the pre-Castro days. If his history was correct, back in 1902 there was an official election in the country which didn't last. Finally President Taft had to send in troops in 1909 to re-establish the Republic. Even then, there were numerous revolutionary and counter-revolutionary groups.

From his research, Arthur has never known of a time when there wasn't trouble in Cuba with groups like this. He tried to trace some current groups to their origins. Without hard data, more of a hand-me-down stories, it appears some of these groups have a long established revolutionary history.

Dante Perez had a brilliant scheme matted out as far as he could see. Begin the popular uprising in the west near Habana and involve the U.S. Perez Guerra and company had already caused great embarrassment to Fidel in several domestic incidents and the international event in New York.

Harrington knew the only action he would see would be them putting a bullet in his head on the way to blow up the refinery. He would be a dead example to prove U.S. involvement. By himself, he didn't know what to do. With some help, he could make things difficult. He had overheard enough to be a threat if he escaped and found help.

Robert Jamison couldn't believe his ears. Rumor had it that the two had escaped. God, he hoped they would materialize instantly in front of his desk to tell him what the hell was going on. There were a lot of pieces to this picture, but the focus was unclear. There had to be some master plan to all the movement and guerilla activity world-wide. The main activity that concerned him was the intelligence reports of activity tying up Cuban commandos world-wide.

To make matters worse, Harrington in Cuba was to check with the pro-American action and report back. He hadn't been heard from. If Harrington could be contacted, he may be able to help clear up matters and get Masters out of Cuba. The suggestion had been made at the last meeting to send someone to help Masters and find Harrington or his body, if dead. The U.S. couldn't risk another incident with the CIA in Cuba. However, sending another person in was just compounding the risk and increasing the probability that someone would be caught. Although his group was not connected to the CIA, their activities elsewhere could be jeopardized.

Robert leaned back in his chair and reminisced to himself about Masters. In covert activities, agents die. But the activities of his group were not like the CIA. His people were used for their brains, to infiltrate with ideas, to engage on an intellectual level. There was occasional hard core undercover work, but on those jobs they were technical advisors to the CIA and the like.

Masters had been with the group for many years, going on 11 in fact. The young politician wasn't originally brought in because of his political expertise. He was a labor union specialist. Penetrating groups' world-wide to spread information, gather information, or to start or stop trouble is often necessary. Union groups world-wide share a certain community of interest or camaraderie. He was often called upon to enter a group and gather information. In numerous cases, he was used to start trouble for the other side to take the heat off U.S. diplomatic mistakes elsewhere.

Masters was a master. His cover had no cracks or leaks. No one guessed his double identity.

Robert smiled, he was never sure that Masters was so good because he was brilliant and had nerves of steel; or because he was so into another world that he didn't realize he could be killed for the kind of activities he performed. Foreign governments under the Soviet tutelage don't take kindly to outsiders, especially Americans, whipping up the anger of the people.

Masters moved around a lot as a young child to many foreign

countries. Fortunately, he learned to speak the languages at his father's urging. The hiatus in Pennsylvania for his later secondary school years balanced the growth pattern.

The political career came along by accident. Masters had become a rather noted labor union supporter and writer in the field. Pennsylvania being a strong union state and having a Governor who needed help for election, Masters was a plum to gather as part of his team.

For the "Research" unit, the political field held real promise for new levels of influence by the agent. Besides, after 10 years of field work at the undercover and danger level, it was in Masters' best interest to move to a different level of involvement.

If Masters did get free, Jamison was convinced of his ability to mix with the locals and find support. Except that Spanish was his weak language. Even at that, he felt there couldn't be a better agent to uncover what was being planned. Once this was discovered, the information would be sent to the hard core spies to remedy.

"Have Masters and the woman been located?"

"No, Dante, but two soldiers spotted them on the highway down from the mountain. The two soldiers were tied up and hidden in the shrub. No telling where they have gone."

"Has the car been found or seen?"

"No, they must have hidden it somewhere."

"The release that she has joined with us in sympathy will be believed till they capture her and they investigate what she says. Then the truth will surface that it was a delay tactic on our part."

"Masters would have been helpful to get Jose' Francia out of jail. But, the Cuban authorities would have none of it. Francia was to be sent to Cuba for Masters. The U.S. officials didn't want him loose in their country. When we or another group find him, he is a dead man. We can't delay our plans. If Masters should escape, someone just may believe him."

"Perez Guerra and the party members from Sierra del Rosario are here now."

"Show them in. We can't stay in this location beyond this meeting. The troops of Fidel could find it to check out the woman's story to the two soldiers. We must make our final arrangements for the attack and move."

The group of radicals moved into the large room in the building across the grass clearing and in front of where Stephen Masters and Joyce Hurtado were kept as prisoners.

Dante began asking persons who were responsible for each area on how things were coming. The group in charge of demolitions was concerned about having enough time to set all the charges. Juan assured them that they would and went over the details of the plan again. Their second concern was if there would be workers hurt who had no part in the plan. Dante expressed regret that some may be hurt, but the larger goal involved justified such risks. However, the late hour the attack was planned meant that only a few workers would be present.

The placement of the dead CIA man was crucial. He must appear to be shot by one of the security guards. Which meant the cover group was to keep the security guard occupied and unaware. Other guards, there are only three for the sugar refinery, could be disposed of.

The demolition crew felt the plan by Juan didn't allow for placement of explosives at enough crucial points around the total facility. With the current plan, only the part of the complex that does the technical refining of the sugar to crystals and the like would be destroyed for certain. It was leaving to chance the rest would be destroyed by spreading fire.

Dante interrupted and mentioned all that is needed is enough fire bombs set to keep the facility out of production. Fancy leveling of the area like an urban renewal detonation was not necessary. It must look like a raid. Hitting swift, inflict damage, and withdraw.

'The CIA man will be placed near the refinery and shot with a security pistol. Then kill the guard near him."

"The refinery is near Matanzas and only about forty miles from Habana, which means our escape is crucial if it is to appear to be a CIA job. All will move south to Gunes then to Batabano. From there to split up Dante's group and Juan's group to move toward Habana and the Sierra del Rosario Mideast. The rest eastward to the retreat near Bayan.

"The troops of Fidel in the eastern region will not send help because of several disturbances that will be set to insure they are held in position. We plan timed explosive devices to be set on army trucks and other vehicles. No direct confrontation, we don't have enough members in our group or equipment at this time. Guerilla tactics will be the techniques. That should also provide sufficient cover to return to the hideouts."

"What of the woman and the American?"

"They are bad property. Who will try to help them now? Both the army as well as the other revolutionary groups are looking for them. A person would be crazy to invite that kind of trouble."

The group seemed in support of the plan and the details were elaborated on as other questions arose. Dante was a good spokesperson. He was charming, reassuring, yet tough. Handsome and rugged in appearance; the kind who would be a politician or do commercials in the U.S. He never did do his own dirty work, and delegated both authority and responsibility to subordinates. With the understanding that failure was not accepted without careful reference to be sure it was beyond the control of the person in charge. Otherwise, the penalty for failure is death.

The trickiest part of the mission was to get from the mountains to and around the city of Matanzas with a group this size. Obvious means of transportation could be used, but carefully and traveling in small numbers. Guns and equipment had to be smuggled in trucks camouflaged among agricultural products where possible.

The timetable for this and the incident in Miami was important. It would take a week to complete the raid on the large sugar refinery. A prize gem of the Castro economic resurgence. The incident in Miami would appear to be swift retaliation. The meeting was only one week after the sugar raid. Plans for it would be completed in the caves near Habana after the sugar refinery raid was a success. If this first part failed, the attempt in Miami may have to wait.

Guerra wanted to lay a trap for the American and the woman. They would be disguised, but recognition would not be difficult. They would probably try to escape by Guantanamo. There are mountains to cover their movements and few roads.

Dante told Guerra to assign their death to the girlfriend of the guard who let them escape.. She seemed committed and without reservation to kill. She could move quickly with two others and wait for them in mountain regions south of Guantanamo. But not to lose time here for her. If the two escapees don't show, quickly join the rest for the raid.

As they went out of the building, the rebel troops were already packing and preparing to move out. The swiftness of the action was evidence of their having moved frequently and with urgency in the past. In a few hours, it would hardly be noticeable that anyone was ever here without more careful examination. The Movemiento Nuevo Politica was well organized and ready to begin their plan to wrestle control from Castro. The swiftness of movement after the Miami incident would require strong leadership in all parts of the island.

Dante had picked members from his group and kept a mental file of leaders of others who could be counted upon. Swift deployment of guerilla tactics and limited confrontation with Castro troops would begin as soon as the American ships began to move into blockade position.

Such a plan is not without many risks and counted upon actions of

parties with no direct interest in
their success, such as the
Americans. But, it was to this group
the quickest and surest way to
overthrow Castro. It would take many
years of persuasion of workers and
disruptive incidents by Dante's
group to use the more standard
formula to seize control by popular
uprising. The swiftest is a military
backed program. But, the military is
prosoviet and their involvement was
not in line with the political
group's objectives.

There was also the support
generated by Jose' Francia from a
segment of the Miami and South
Florida Cuban population. While some
Cubans escaped with their wealth,
most fled leaving families and
property behind. The wealthy Cubans

might be convinced to help if it meant the return of their property in their homeland that with Castro became part of the state owned and divided up parcels. The radical wing of their movement had failed to win support of the masses of Cubans and other Latins. But, greed and bloodlines run along similar thinking patterns. As the revolution took hold, money and support would be forthcoming Dante was sure.

Chapter 8
ON TO GET THERE

The rest was needed and we both awoke with no sleepy side effects. There would be no time for drowsy or dimwit actions.

Joyce sat scratching something in the dirt near where we slept. I asked her why she decided to retreat into her childhood and play now. She called me over and said there was a way to get out by going down the southern edge of the mountains to Guantanamo for our escape.

I looked at her and reminded her of the plan that Dante told us about concerning the sugar refinery. We couldn't just let that happen. I didn't have any terrific suggestions as such, but did feel the necessity

to try to stop it. Going down south
to escape would take valuable time.

"The role model for individuals
in our society is to fend for
themselves. We have whole economic
theories based on self-interest
actions. So why is a 'capitalist'
raised person interested in saving a
sugar refinery and my socialist
counterpart going after her own
well-being?"

"Because, my 'capitalist'
friend, it is more than likely to be
impossible to get across the
country. The police and the
underground both search for us. I
don't believe you really care for
some poor people and a pile of sugar
cane."

"Let's put it this way, Joyce, America seldom does anything correct in foreign affairs. We have this big, beautiful self-image of ourselves as a 'Dutch uncle' to the world. But, in reality, our actions are like a young 'toddler' tripping over his own feet. We oppose war but we sell weapons to both sides and rationalize it's for the adequate defense of both parties. The rest of the world views such actions with disdain. Soon a CIA man is going to be executed and it will be made to look like he is the key person in this plot. I don't want to see our faces covered with mud again, especially without our being involved to deserve the mud pile treatment."

"Not involved! What the hell is a CIA man doing in Cuba to begin with? You pompous Yankee politician."

"What about the Cuban groups in the U.S. Joyce? Is that okay?"

"Everyone is in the U.S. Of course it's okay. Hell, the world owns the U.S. industries, your armies are illiterate, your welfare rolls include one out of every three households and you're head over heels in debt, but your Congress just spends what it must to get re-elected. It would be crazy for other countries not to be over there spying. My God, you've got a war arsenal with the trip finger held by a leader that changes opinion based on what group he's speaking to."

"I don't agree that he's that bad. But, if so, do you want this scenario played out with the second step in Miami and for real problems to mushroom?"

"No, but I still don't know how we can get across fifty percent of the country without being caught. What do we do when we get there? You're no James Bond and I'm not Wonder Woman."

"My, aren't we negative. Some food and a little coffee will pick up your spirits. Besides, Dante must be expecting us to go toward Guantanamo."

We took off on foot toward the village. Joyce was dressed enough like a farm worker to go in and get a few items. The money was by courtesy of the soldiers in the jeep. I stayed outside the village. Six foot blondes don't pass themselves off as Cubans very well.

While we ate, I tried on the floppy cloth hat she found to hide my hair. It wasn't attractive, but it would do. We agreed to try to make our way via an illegal ride on a train. Cuba has some 11,000 odd miles of railroad. Mostly in poor condition. But, it should still be faster than walking, and safer than stealing another vehicle.

We figured about a five mile hike to pick up a railroad line that would connect with the main east-west lines at Marti. The ride would carry us through Camaguey, principal city of the province named the same and on to Ciego de Avila beyond which we hoped to go north to Santa Clara and east through Colon, Jovellanos, and finally to Matanzas, the site of the raid.

However, the trains don't always run on schedule or where one wants them to when you're hiding in box cars like a hobo. We felt confident we'd be able to find a schedule at Marti, the first real city on the route to Matanzas. The next problem was to avoid being noticed in the terminals and when the train stopped to be loaded or unloaded.

Cuba's climate is generally favorable and modified by sea breezes. Yet, as one moved inland, the humidity became uncomfortable and the box cars would be hot.

We found the line and began walking the tracks. We walked five miles to even get there and had gone another three miles before we heard the first sounds of an oncoming train. As slow as it was moving would be a help for us to board. But it's still tricky to jump aboard a moving vehicle. Thank God we're not in France where they move at high speeds.

While walking along the railroad tracks, we tried to verbalize some form of action plan to use when we got closer to our destination. As would be expected, the conversation would drift away from our 'solution'. Especially since there were so many potential variables that could change the preconceived action plan. One obvious variable is the belief that we can hitch a ride from here to Matanzas, another is how much time we'd have. For all we know, it could take us one day or six days to go this relatively short trip.

Walking the railroad line also evoked childhood memories for both of us. It must be universal fun for children to play on these damn things. To see if you can balance yourself on the track itself. I always imagined myself to be a circus high wire performer. Joyce thought of herself as a fox running along the iron track.

The total eight mile hike took us some three hours. Hardly an Olympic walking record, but we didn't want to get caught, so we tried to be cautious until we reached the railroad line. The line followed the road for a short distance. Then it separated and went into the country.

I thought to myself how proud Robert Jamison would be of me. Joyce had a good argument to go south. If I felt sure we could get help quickly and without causing the Cuban authorities to appear, it would have been a good idea. That feeling not being the case, the best alternative was to go and try to save a sugar refinery on our own. Being on the job in this capacity for me was not in my normal operating mode. This bordered on the more physical side of the job. The side not to my preference. There have been tight situations before. In those cases it involved a mass of people causing trouble, or a small group getting information. In any case, it always seemed that I had a support base to work from and more familiar environment to operate amidst. Objectives were never of the paramilitary type - such as stopping raids on refineries. As such, the use of force was always a last resort alternative.

The research unit under Jamison's direction used words and ideas as our weapons. They were effective weapons when used properly. The idea was borrowed from the Russians. They have been using people in various parts of the world to stir up trouble for years. At the research unit, it was known when instigators were planted by the Russians to stir up trouble. Now we were using their tactics. From what we learned, they didn't like the idea at all.

We hid where the brush was closest to the track to make the jump unnoticed. My stomach churned with fear. Just knowing I could fall or trip and be smashed under a train. My God, what a way to die! An ignoble demise along a railroad in the back country of Cuba because I was too clumsy to hop aboard a slow moving box car.

Joyce asked what we were to do if they didn't leave the doors wide open. I never thought of that. Hell, they're always open in the movies. Have faith was the only thing my mind could muster as a response to her. Her retort was that faith is a Judo-Christian phenomenon, and poor peoples of the socialist world have used up their quota long ago.

We spotted a car coming that appeared to have the doors open. As the car approached, I held her under the shoulders and shoved. She grabbed the door with her right hand and clawed the floor of the car with the left to climb in. Meanwhile, I was chugging alongside trying to watch the car and the ground at the same time to keep from falling.

"Hurry up dimwit she yelled!"

I grabbed the door and pulled up and in. Relief! If only this dirty little car would go the entire trip to Matanzas.

The car was not empty. It contained some tobacco and fruit, mangos to be precise. I grabbed the oblong, slightly acid tasting fruit and began to eat. The juice served as a source of refreshment and raised my sunken blood sugar level.

We leaned against the side of the boxcar near the door and slid my back flat along the wall and went to a sitting position. Being near the door gave some breeze as well as light. I took my new hat off to wipe away the sweat from my forehead. The band inside the hat was soaked so I left the hat off to dry out. Hats always leave an indentation around my head, just above my ears. Sort of a ring around the head. A mirror would be nice about now to see how bad it looked.

My paranoia over my hair annoyed Joyce. She promptly referred to me as an egocentric asshole. It was

useless to explain my fears about
'ring around the head' to her, so I
kept eating mangos. The only hope is
they do not cause diarrhea. That was
the last thing either of us needed
today

The trip was slow and uneventful
through Marti and on toward
Camaguey. At Camaguey, it looked
like a large freight yard was the
destination.. We opted to get out of
the car versus waiting and proceed
through the city to pick up another
freight on the other side heading
toward Ciego de Avila, on-route to
our destination. The car we were in
may well wait for a long period to
be unloaded or to move on. We took
several mangos along and began to
wind our way out of the freight yard
as inconspicuously as possible.

Besides, waiting in freight yards is a way to get caught by freight yard inspectors.

Camaguey was an old provincial town that has fallen into bad times since the Castro takeover. What was once many proud and bright stucco buildings, were now in need of repair and paint? We cut across the city by walking with a group of persons heading home for the evening. During the walk it was hard to fathom all the old cars that were in use. Almost like a movie set taking place back 15-20 years in time. Oh well it did help our cover with the crowd of workers and the afternoon dusk helped form a natural way to proceed to the railroad tracks.

We picked up the railroad track heading for the small city of Florida, which is about twenty miles west of Camaguey.

"I don't think we're going to get a train tonight. Maybe we should find a place to rest. I'm tired. We must have walked three miles!" Joyce replied.

"After we get further from the city Steve. It's too close Here. Another couple of miles we should be safe. There are some streams that feed the small river that flows near Florida. It will be cooler there."

Joyce was correct. We did find a little stream just off the track. The spot was protected from view by trees and dense foliage around what appeared like my favorite swimming 'hole' as a kid. Back in Pennsylvania our gang would swim at a spot that resembled this one. We had a huge oak that had a rope with a tire tied to it. We would swing out and jump in the water. What a shame, that incredible spot for fun is now a development. Kids in that area now go to a municipal pool.

Our society continues to choke the creative process of our youth. Then this same society becomes angered when the youth are at a loss for entertainment when we close the pools, supervised parks and ball fields for some legitimate reason. We've systematically removed these 'perfect' spots of mind expanding fun and discovery and replaced them with controlled environments.

I stripped and waded in to cool off and clean off. It felt so good after the hot dusty trip on the train and the events of the day and night before. A bar of soap would have made it all complete.

Joyce spent the first twenty minutes fixing a place to rest that would be well hidden. Then much to my delight she joined me for a 'skinny dip' in the water. She was rubbing herself all over and trying as I did to bathe without soap. The water was refreshing. After ten or so minutes she spoke, apparently revived and cheerful.

"Joyce, I don't think I can survive on mangos for too long. Have any ideas what we can eat?" She looked at me, smiled and spoke.

"Good Lord, I must look bad when all you can think of is mangos when I'm naked in the water beside you."

"I'm trying not to be an animal about it."

"That didn't bother you back at the camp."

"I thought we were going to die. It was a symbolic last supper of sorts."

"Very peculiar 'of sorts' I'd say."

I held her close and began to kiss her forehead, nose and lips. The erotic idea of making love in the water began to take its effect. Who would need more food? Mangos would be just fine.

When we finished lovemaking in the water, we headed for the stream bank to get some sleep.

"We'll have to sleep in the buff, I washed our clothes out."

"My whole body is alive now. Nothing, food or clothes, will matter."

"Relax, we need sleep. It's a long trip to Matanzas my boy."

"Boy?"

"Steve - I hear something. Wake up!"

I jumped from the rustic shelter and stubbed my toe on a rock.

"You look funny hopping and screaming in the nude with your 'manhood' dancing about."

I didn't swear at Joyce. It all goes back to my upbringing that offers an attitude of respect for a woman you've slept with. But she was pushing that to the limit.

The sound was a train. We dressed frantically in the slightly damp apparel and waited along the track. The hopping aboard was smoother this time, but inside the car was a different story. Although it was empty, it had been used to haul pigs. Nothing smells worse than pig shit. I thought I would lose what remained of the fruit in my stomach.

We kicked away what shit we could from the floor near the door and rode with our faces out the opening. Dangerous, yes, but necessary to keep from passing out.

The train took us through Ciego de Avila, stopping just briefly there and at Jatibonico to load and unload some cargo. We couldn't tell exactly what was being done for fear of lumbering out of the freight car and being caught.

From Jatibonico, the train went into Sancti-Spiritus, its apparent destination. Apparent because the thing shut down and cars were being separated and the overall type of movement was not indicative of heading where we wanted to go.

This part of Cuba contained the Sierra Trinidad mountain range with some fairly high peaks by the standards of an easterner. That is, in the area of 3,500 feet. The many caves and isolated valley offer more potential for the revolutionary faction to hide.

From what Joyce could learn, the tracks leading north were in a state of disrepair almost to Santa Clara. The train trip for this period would be longer than we wanted to take, but cutting across the mountains could be dangerous exposure to unfriendly groups and time consuming by foot.

There are field work crews that go to different large farms to harvest crops. They meet at pick-up points and travel to their destination. Joyce was locating the best place for us to mix in with the work crowd to hitch a ride. I sat on the ground and tried not to look obvious, Christ, I was hungry.. I was contemplating stealing a worker's sack but thought the unnecessary attention might be harmful if I was caught in the act.

The right pickup spot was located, and I moved to sit there. Joyce had also bought some bread and fruit. We ate and sat quiet. I hoped they didn't call role or whatever.

"Steve, you don't need to park your ass everywhere in order not to stick out. Cubans are not short people."

"Thanks, I hate to stereotype, but all Latins, Mexicans, Cubans whatever, all bring visions of little tan skinned people in white outfits with big straw hats to me."

"Yankee jerk."

We boarded the bus without incident and took our seats. The bus headed north. The trip would take us over a mountain past Fomento and near Placetas. This would be an ideal location near Santa Clara to catch the train for the last leg of the trip to Matanzas.

I have always enjoyed riding in the country and enjoying the scenery. Despite the ominous threat of international incident that need be stopped, I still loved the ride. It must be a throwback to the joy of riding on the numerous Pennsylvania country roads. They all go somewhere, sometimes in circles, but they fit the bill to get the Pennsylvania farmers out of the mud. A fulfillment of a Governor's promise, if elected that is, long ago. The country farmer would be provided with paved roads to get their crops to market. The bumps, ruts and jostling on this road tended to keep me from sleeping, so the sightseeing gave me a chance to relax and try to figure out what the hell to do to stop the plot to implicate the U.S. government.

Joyce slept. I don't know how. God, she is beautiful! There was this deep desire to cuddle her close while she slept. However, on a migrant worker transport bus was not the place to express my emotions.

The trouble with the time to reflect and think is that it tends to let you rationalize yourself out of things. Things like trying to stop a plot by yourself against a small revolutionary mini-army. Talking to myself, the conversation went, let's be rational, would the

Habana government _really_ believe this is all part of a master U.S. plan to create insurrection in Cuba? Would the U.S. government really believe the following plan in Miami is Castro's revenge? The whole dream scenario of Perez may be just that - a pipe dream. God, a U.S. blockade of Cuba. Can you imagine!

I looked out the bus window and scratched my head. The trouble is, yes. We did invade Cuba before in a master plot to dethrone Castro. We had a blockade before. It could all just be crazy enough to happen. Maybe not to the dream scale of Perez, but enough to cost many lives and tighten already tedious world problems and fan anti-U.S. sentiment in the southern hemisphere. The problems in El Salvadore and the support of Britain in the Faulkland Island war haven't made the United States a beloved neighbor.

Joyce elbowed me in the side rather sharply.

"Shut up, you're babbling in English and we're getting some strange looks." She was upset and tried to speak with her teeth shut.

"I didn't realize I was talking aloud."

It was dark till we reached Santa Clara and we were herded like sheep into large huts. The accommodations were not the best, quite primitive in design and construction. My main problem was finding the bathroom. The jostling of my kidneys and other parts put me in dire need of facilities.

Fortunately, I remembered the word for bathroom and was directed where to go. Thank God the guy pointed while he spoke or I never would have figured out the whereabouts of the tin covered 'mecca'.

As expected, it was not modern, indoor, but primitive style of yesteryear. I imagined all sorts of things were about to crawl on me, but it did suffice.

Sleeping would be an easy task, despite the hunger. I was exhausted and tomorrow would be the important push for us to reach Matanzas. Time was running out to stop the Perez plan. Three days would be up and it would take another to get to the refinery.

Chapter 9
HOW TO FIND IT

When we awoke, it was still
dark. The human mind must have its
own little alarm clock. We didn't
have a clock, but needed to be up
and away before the others were
ready.

The big drawback was missing
breakfast. No matter what it may
taste like, when you're hungry, it's
good.

We walked out of the area onto
the road to get our bearings. From
what we could tell, we were a few
miles west of Santa Clara. Our
options were a little better than
before, but still no direct route to
our destination. We could take the
scenic route by river, the slow
route by train or steal a car.

The scenic route involves the rivers near Matanzas. The Yumuri River has produced some of the most picturesque beauty in the tropics. The erosion patterns have created steep canyon-like walls, almost 500 feet in some places, along the rivers in that area. Some of the rivers are navigable for short distances by small boats. While I opted to see the area of rich tropical scenery, Joyce was quick to point out that it was impractical and very slow.

Stealing a car could result in being caught, but it was quick and a more direct route.

Fidel has been in the process of connecting the largest cities on the island by way of an eight lane super-highway across the center of the country. Using it would cut our trip from days to ten hours. However, the highway is patrolled by the military and a stolen car would be quickly uncovered in a country with few cars to begin with. The obvious goal of the highway is to facilitate commerce and make up for the poor condition of the railroad. Making the railroad a priority instead of the roads would not generate the volume of jobs or facilitate the level of commerce envisioned by the Castro government.

Well, it's back to the train. Joyce won out with boring logic.

"Why are you so strange? You know we don't have time to float down some river."

"I'm hungry, I guess."

"You seem to be losing the purpose of the mission and why we are here instead of trying to get out through the southeast."

"You're right." My voice and its tone were that of an upset and tired person. "I'm hungry, tired, and need a bath, Let's go, Joyce."

The railroad area was bordered on the south by a small mountainous area, thick with vegetation. Its other side was the more flat areas that moved out to the Atlantic, almost uninterrupted and excellent for farming.

We proceeded along the side of dense vegetation to cover our movements as much as possible. The trip was slow and hot. No trains came our way and it was about noon time. A half day lost,

We were resting in a clearing when we heard a train coming. As with the others, the condition of the tracks dictated that the speed would be slow enough to board. As it approached, we picked out a car that looked open about midway in the train. I helped Joyce jump on and started my run alongside to get in. The ground next to the tracks sloped downward at an angle away from the elevated track making running difficult, which resulted in my falling. I wanted to sit and recover, but had to catch up with Joyce in the car. Ahead, about 200 yards, was a bridge. I had to board before that or get another car. I ran as fast as I could without falling again, only I heard some strange yelling in the car. The noise of the train drowned out the voices not allowing me to hear clearly. When I caught up with the train and started to climb in, I knew why the noise. Our car was occupied by a trio of men. Not the old time knights of the road that we have in America, but rough-looking characters that belong to one of the underground groups.

One has to move quickly in these cases. I planned to hop in and grab one. But they think fast also. Just as I rolled in, one kicked me in the face and the other was on me in a flash. The third was on the floor wrestling with Joyce.

The train took a favorable shift around a turn and I was able to get the fellow off me. While rolling him off and trying to stand up, I kept a firm grasp on his shirt and threw him out the door. As he flew, his body went out and hit a tree with the small of his back. The tree didn't break so it must have been his back that made the cracking noise. The one that kicked me had a knife out and was coming at full speed.

Although I was now by trade a politician, my youth was ill spent in pool halls and similar establishments. Fighting was not unknown to me, especially the street variety. I jumped away and took off the poncho to use as protection. Joyce was holding her own, sort of. She had taken some hard hits in the face, but was able to occupy the assailant. I hoped she could hold on for just a few minutes more.

She screamed when the fellow kicked her in the side. My attacker looked for a split second and that was all I needed. The poncho went over his head. I kicked him in the groin and grabbed the poncho and ran his head into the side of the rail car. I kept smashing it till blood poured out through the poncho and down onto the floor of the car. He was next to be thrown out the car and I went over to help Joyce.

Her assailant turned as I came over across the car. A jolt on the rough tracks sent me stumbling toward him. A bad turn of events for me. I took another hard knock to the face. It would be two weeks till I could chew hard food again. The earlier kick and this punch felt like it loosened all the teeth in my lower left jaw. Joyce, God bless her, rallied and grabbed him from the back and I began punching him violently. I stopped when he seemed half dead. We let him drop to the floor to find out some idea why we were attacked. My hysterical screaming of questions at him seemed to get nowhere. Joyce asked him in Spanish. That seemed to work. He told us both the government and Dante had rewards out for us. Being alive was not a necessary condition for collecting. My ears couldn't believe what he was saying. A violent attack like this. My anger flew into a blind rage and I threw him out of the car head first,

"My God, are you okay?" Joyce took some hard blows to the face. The red marks on the right side would soon turn to large bruises. Her right side was bruised and she thought some ribs had been broken. But to me it felt more like the cartilage between them had been cracked.

"I hurt. I don't feel good and I don't like to cry." She was hurt and in obvious pain. I hate to see people I care for in pain and I tried to comfort her.

"Don't worry about it. Let's check you out to be sure there are no other breaks or concussion."

"You're hurt. Your face is cut and your lip is huge. Is your eye okay? It looks like it will swell shut soon."

"It probably will, but that is nothing new. Lay down and let me clean you up: Our 'wrecking' crew left their water cartons and food. This may sting as I clean these marks, but relax."

I proceeded to clean Joyce up, gave her some food and got her comfortable. She was in deep pain from the assault. I looked worse but with a cool rag and a little luck the swelling would come down a little by the next day.

Eating their stuff was difficult on just one side of the mouth, but I was starved. We found as comfortable a position as possible and rested. My stomach was in knots. I kept trying to figure why we tried this crazy scheme to save some sugar refinery. We took a nap for about an hour or so and woke up to some strange noise outside. The train had stopped.

Joyce crawled near the door to listen.

"The military stopped the train. There has been some trouble ahead. We are to get troops to ride with the engineer and on the back."

"What kind of trouble Joyce?"

"Terrorist. They have sabotaged tracks on the other side of Colon. The train will have to stop there for the night."

"Was this train headed to Matanzas?"

"No, just to Jovellanos."

"Where the hell is that?"

"About forty miles from Matanzas."

"Dammit. Well that's alright, it will be night till we get there the way it looks."

"Steve, we better hide in here in case they check the cars. These boxes can be arranged if we're quick."

I didn't know either of us could move anything. For that matter, how we won the fight was a miracle. It always amazes me what the human body can accomplish when pushed.

We moved enough of the boxes of packed fruit to make a spare in the back. Right next to a big rat. He looked mean and didn't want to leave, I crawled on top of a box and threw a small carton at it. I never saw a rat jump before, but this one jumped at me. "Holy shit, what kind of rats do you have in Cuba?"

"Shush or we'll be heard."

"Shush - did you learn that eloquent prose at Penn State? I've got a militant rat trying to throw me out and what help are you?"

"Watch." She took a piece of board that is used to stack between layers of boxes and started swinging at the culprit. The rat scurried for the front. Joyce followed up with a beautiful ground shot and sent him out of the car. We quickly headed for the hiding spot with the club and other paraphernalia that might give away our presence.

"Let me move these boxes overhead. The slats will support a couple of boxes over top of us and make it look like its solid boxes on here."

The strategy paid off. The flying rat attracted the attention of a soldier. He climbed in the car. We peeked as best we could.

"Captain,"

"Si"

"Look at this, it looks like blood."

"Help me into the car."

"I don't see anything else but boxes, but this is fresh blood on the side of the car."

"Yes, there were two dead men found back the route earlier beside the tracks. They could have been involved. Both were part of the underground against Fidel, Check all the cars very thoroughly, and radio ahead to stop all trains through Colon to look for illegal riders.

"Si Captain, but isn't it unusual for guerillas to be in this part of the country and that close to Habana?"

You are correct. I don't understand, but conduct the search, there may be more on board the train."

We sat for what seemed like forever after the soldiers left the car. I took my pulse once. Without a watch. I'm not sure how fast per minute the beats were, but it was pounding like hell.

"Have they gone?"

"I don't know", I whispered to her, "but I think I. will stay here till Colon. If you don't mind."

"What are we going to do in Colon?"

"You're the local expert. I had hoped you might know your way around."

"You're wrong. I've been to Colon only once and that was as a little girl."

"Oh shit."

"That's not nice. Besides, I didn't mean 'I didn't know directions. What I meant was what

are we going to do to get off this
train without getting caught?"

"I don't know yet. Let's hope
things sort of flow our way." "Well,
if earlier was an example, then
things aren't flowing too smoothly."

"Have I ever told you that you
sound like a wife at times?"

"That's your stereotype
capitalist attitude. Women in free
socialist environments don't sound
like wives. We are treated equal and
don't need amendments to achieve
what is inherently ours."

"Is this paid for by some party
or just some free propaganda that I
alone am privileged to hear? Tell
me, I never read or heard of
terrorist attacks in the papers or

201

radio Cuba. Is this suppression part of the free socialist press?"

The train began moving and I could sense one of our ideological semi-arguments coming along.

"Your free press in America is made of irresponsible generalists that write about topics and conditions they are unqualified to discuss. Only a fraction are trained in any specialty. The best reporting is by writers in sports, housekeeping, business and bridge. The terrorist reports are suppressed to keep from glorifying the acts and creating heroes out of renegades."

"Jesus."

"Whitty answer for a politician."

"You didn't let me finish."

"Before I give you equal time, let's decide how we are going to get off this train and how to get around Cuba."

"Don't change the subject."

"I promised you equal time later."

"But the spontaneity of the moment will be lost."

"It already is lost."

The rest of the trip to Colon was spent in our little space hiding and arguing over trivial political questions, The train moved at a snail's pace and it was dark till we arrived,

Getting off the train and out of the yard was not as difficult as we earlier feared. The fruit had to be unloaded before spoilage took place

203

and there was a small army of workers at the train scurrying boxes to waiting trucks·. Mixing in with the work crew wasn't difficult; unloading and carrying when you're tired, hungry and sore from being in a fight is difficult.

After the unloading, we walked with the work crew and caught a bus ride to the northwest edge of town.

Not your typical metro bus - another of those work transports - although I must say the inside of this had less graffiti and the people were more polite than in a U.S. city.

Joyce spoke as we walked from the bus. "You know, there was some merit to your point about not hearing of revolutionaries in Cuba."

"Suppression of the news?"

"No, Fidel had a special plan, or 'plan number two' as it was called. The plan was to remove the revolutionary bands from the mountain region of Las Villas and Pinar del Rio provinces. Fidel removed the problem by depopulating the areas. When the bandits were without local peasantry to supply food, money, and clothes, the bands of revolutionaries left.

"Are you saying the locals supported these people?"

"Yes, they were seen as sort of . . oh. . uh. . like your Robin Hood and his Merry Men. If you remember the Vietnam situation. Who was the base of support for the North Vietnamese?"

"It was the local villagers."

"It was the same thing here."

"That was in the mid to late sixties, Steve. Now, the bandits are cropping up again."

"Any reason why the resurgence of counter revolutionaries'?"

"Oh, a few. Fidel has not been able to deliver quick enough on some of his promises for economic growth. The poor are much better off than they ever have been, but around thirty to forty percent of the population has been born since the revolution in 1959. Their expectations are much higher than their peasant parents. Concrete huts and farm cooperatives are not enough. They want more and don't always share the same lack of respect of the older generation for the Americans. It's not all Fidel's fault. Droughts, technical problems, financing troops worldwide, all demand money and time or are out of his control."

It's sort of like our labor movement in America. The older generations remember the abuse and exploitation by managers and owners of industry. Now, the younger workers have it damn good. They don't see the necessity to join unions or be militant about key job issues.

We walked about a mile or so and were tired from an active day of fear and physical abuse. This is one of the few times in my life when I can remember not having vivid sexual fantasies when looking for a place to spend the night with a beautiful woman.

"Is that a cottage ahead? It looks deserted."

Hut was the more appropriate term. When we moved closer, it was almost ready to fall down from years of neglect. A small square structure with a louvered front door and windows. None of which still held all their hinges. The wood porch and outer walls were once white, now a dirty and weathered gray. The tile roof was still intact with a great deal of vegetation growing among the half found tiles. Hidden by the moss and weeds almost to the point of acceptable camouflage if viewed from above. One could still picture the bygone process by which these roof tiles were made. The shape conforming to the thigh of the person who was responsible. Each roof tile individually made by placing the clay over the person's thigh to get the barrel shape. The unfortunate part comes in the future when repairs to the broken tiles are needed. Without the original maker's thigh for a mold, duplication is impossible.

We peered through the door. The walls were stucco and the floor wooden. But not in disrepair as was the outside of the house. Almost as if the desire was to discourage anyone from bothering to approach the hut,

"Oh no, we better leave here Steve, this is not a place we want to be."

"What the hell is all of this junk? It looks <u>similar to an</u> altar of sorts."

"It is an altar. A voodoo altar."

"I thought that this sort of thing was limited to Haiti."

"Well, in Cuba the cult is Santeria, very similar to other island offshoots. Jamaica is the pocomania. The same idea in Trini'-dad is named after Yoruba the thunder god,"

"You must be kidding. The literacy rate in Cuba is too high for this shit Joyce. You people may not believe in God - but voodoo!"

"I don't, but much of Cuba's population is of, African descent. Old rituals die hard, Steve."

"Should we say 'Adios' to this place and scat?"

"That's cute Steve, Let's say hasta la vista instead and not push our luck as go with God may not be appreciated; worse yet, it may be confusing. There must be symbols of ten gods here."

"Oh hell, we're in for a difficult time. Here come some visitors this way."

"Where do we hide, Steve?"

"I don't live here. Hell if I know. Let's try and find a back door or window."

Joyce ran to check the rest of the hut. "No luck, there isn't either."

"OK, under here and let's be as quiet as a voodoo mouse." "Cute, hide under the covering flap of the altar! What if they pull it back or whatever?"

"I will wait under there until you offer a better place to go."

The flap tacked across the altar was a heavy burlap with figures of creatures painted on it. The space behind was wide enough to sit sideways with legs bent and knees under our chins.

The altar was against the far wall to the right as one entered the front door and was entire width of the hut. We both peered through slits in the material to witness this event and to have a first-hand knowledge if our presence was detected. thought to myself - please don't sneeze, cough, get a cramp, burp or whatever.

The event began in a slow fashion with some candles being lit and the group singing. Almost resembling a Catholic church ceremony. The hougan, or priest, started sprinkling water on the ground and the group of people. There were about six or so people and three drummers, plus the hougan. The group was sitting on the floor with their legs back under their buttocks. While they were not in any fancy outfits, they all were similarly dressed in very dark clothes and ponchos. After the water, the pace picked up to a faster and tumultuously loud level. The strident high pitched chanting of the group almost seemed impromptu, except that all were chanting the same beat.

The commanding voice of the priest standing in front of the group with his back to the altar and us rang out a different line and everything stopped for a moment. In the front door two men dragged in another man. The fellow dragged in was a soldier. They placed him on the floor with his dead propped over a large round clay pot.

The drums rang out again, this time accompanied by uninhibited dancing of several of the group around the soldier. This went on until the whole group seemed hypnotized by the repetitions of the complex sound and rhythm patterns.

My eyes were wide from astonishment of what I was witnessing. One has seen recreations of these events in movies and on T.V., all the time assuming it to be nice theatrics. Never would it enter my mind it could all be so true.

I looked at Joyce to see if she shared the same reaction. She quit watching and was merely trying to stay motionless. I nodded my head for her to watch again.

One of the dancers was going into such a trance that the strong screams of the priest seemed to stagger him and all his sense of reality was leaving. I found that I was having difficulty in dealing with the whole process and had to stuff torn pieces of clothing in my ears to cut out some of the noise and keep my own perspective.

The end result seemed apparent. The soldier on the floor would be a human sacrifice. His life taken by the dancer who was the most involved in the hypnotic trance.

I couldn't let that happen. I had an idea and tried to tell Joyce by hand signals what was to transpire. Her return looks were not of confidence but accepting my Judo Christian necessity to stop the apparent sacrifice.

The moment for us to act was near. Suddenly there was an intrusive shift in the stable rhythmic dimension of the event. The hypnotic dancer was handed a knife by the priest and the dancer straddled the frightened soldier.

The altar top was a counter-type arrangement that was only laid on top of what resembled three tall carpenter's horses. With as much speed and clamor as possible, we both stood up with the altar top rising.

The confused drummers were the first to clear the room, followed quickly by the others except for the priest, the dancer, and of course, the soldier.

The effect was perfect. It was as if a voodoo god had come to life in front of their eyes. Candles and oil lanterns went crashing to the floor along with dozens of clay pots, dishes and figures of god-like creatures.

The old wooden structure was quick to catch fire and with help of spilled oil it moved quickly through the hut. We heaved the altar at the priest and dancer and sent them to the floor. We rescued the soldier and dragged him outside with us.

The hut was a dazzling blaze that lit up the entire area. We had to get out of there quickly before attention was focused on that vicinity and our presence there discovered,

Our soldier friend, sufficiently recovered to move on his own, led us down the road and into a field where his jeep was sitting. We got in and he drove us away from the spot of potential trouble.

I asked him what the hell that was all about. He didn't speak English. I felt stupid and angry. Joyce translated my question and his answer.

"He shot a boy for stealing. The boy was presumed to be a loas, or godlike, with ability to tell the future. The family of people felt the soldier angered the gods and revenge in the form of his sacrifice was the answer."

"Tell him to watch the road Joyce, we're about to get killed here. He doesn't need to look at me and nod his head while you talk." It must be a similar trait of Latins and similar groups. The same type mental approach I remembered in Italy. All the drivers look the other way.

"He says he is in our debt. He knows who we are from the reports and can help us tonight, but then we are on our own."

"Can he take us to Matanzas?"

"No, but to Jovellanos, plus he can get us a place to stay there, food and some money, and his silence."

"That sounds like a good deal to me. Hey, does he know where the refinery is in Matanzas?"

"Yes, and no. You see, there are numerous refineries there. We have to figure out which one."

"I thought they were like oil refineries."

"They are just less expensive to build. That's why there are more of them."

"Let's relax till we get to Jovellanos. There is no sense getting upset now."

Chapter 10
LOOKING IT OVER

"Gracias Senor,"

"Oh, Steve, we don't say senor or senora anymore. They have given way to companero or compaiiera. Roughly translated, it means comrade. It displays the equality of the socialistic system."

"Bullshit. You don't actually believe all these superficial accommodations really change anything*"

"Wealth is not a class factor in Cuba anymore."

I looked at Joyce and couldn't hold back my sharp response. "No it isn't, but power is a way to judge the difference. And, you must admit, that it has been substituted for money as a way to classify and rank your citizens - comrade."

"There are certain arguments to be offered along those lines, but the real issue is to get some sleep. We have to find our refinery in the morning."

A smile came across my face. I won this argument and she knew it. "Uh-huh, got ya, and you don't want to keep the debate going."

"I can see why 'macho' is a Latin concept that hasn't been completely integrated into America. Macho is also a state of mind, not a child-like attitude."

Our evening stay in Jovellanos was another hut. This time without the voodoo entertainment. Unlike many huts in Cuba, this one possessed all the basic creature comforts. Electricity and running water. The hot water was via a solar heating device on the roof. Judging from the storage tank and other parts, built around 1920 and still working. The shower felt good and the food, what could be chewed, was excellent.

We both took the opportunity to wash out our clothes and hang them up to dry. Our soldier friend was gone. He had to get to his station for the night. The but was his families, that is, a brother and sister-in-law, who were away. His brother was substantially smaller than I, so my evening attire was a poncho like garment that buttoned up the front. Joyce wore a shirt.

"Don't kiss so hard Joyce. My lip is still sore and my teeth are not back in place yet." Joyce found this humorous and began to laugh at me. "There is no reason to laugh. I'll give you a reason to laugh. Didn't you ever hear of the "mad tickler" from Pennsylvania?"

It was an interesting relationship with Joyce. We could engage in continual banter, yet forget the politics to relax. My guess was because neither of us believed our own arguments to any significant extent. By my way of thinking, America was the best of all worlds. But it was a long way from perfect and nowhere near the point of devout religious-like respect some grant it.

My Cuban diplomatic adventure mate was unbelievably sensuous in her shirt nightie. As I tickled her, the shirt rose exposing a cute bare bottom. A little pain in kissing could be handled. She was too lovely to pass up.

The next hours passed in delightful foreplay and lovemaking. During which, we spoke quietly, without political banter, and held each other. The calming and relaxing effect of holding another person is tremendous. We both agreed it was excellent therapy. Late that night, we fell asleep while holding each other and didn't awaken till morning in the same relative position. An uncommon occurrence for me to sleep that soundly.

Breakfast with coffee was a delightful change from the past days of going hungry. Our clothes were dry enough to wear and the overall feeling of being fed, clean, and relaxed gave us both an assured confidence to keep on with the mission.

Although we still couldn't get over the voodoo ritual the other night, Joyce was not surprised that superstition was present in Cuba, but in that extreme degree it is usually associated with Haiti.

Our soldier friend said his brother had a motorcycle. He didn't know how well it ran, but if we use it, make sure he can get it back. We weren't sure how to return it, but we would try to leave a message where it could be located.

The cycle was an old Indian. A relic from the era of WW II. But it did run. A sort of sad commentary for today's products. This would be a marked change in transportation modes for us. No dirty bus or jumping on trains.

"Do they have a helmet law in Cuba?"

"What?"

"Do they have a helmet law in Cuba?" I didn't want to be stopped for something stupid like not wearing a helmet.

"Americans...drive on Stephen, there is no helmet law that I know of in Cuba."

"Where do I drive to? I'm not from Jovellanos?"

Joyce began to motion with her hands which way to go. "Up this way and go straight till you come to Matanzas. We are just off the main road. When you get to it, take a right and go straight."

"Gracias companera." It was a perfect response to start the day off on the right foot of constant banter.

It felt like being back in my late teens in college; cruising about on a cycle with a gal on the back holding on. The road we took was not the main central highway of Cuba. But it was still not bad. A two-lane affair with modest amount of repair needed.

The ride let me recount what the soldier told us about Matanzas. It was in the province of the same name. To the south was the swamp area of Cienaga de Zapata, and to the north, northwest were hilly ranges rising to around 1100 feet in the Pan de Matanzas. The province and city were in the beautiful Yumuri valley area with the Belamar Caves.

The city was founded around 1693 and had approximately 85,000 to 100,000 people. It was bordered by three rivers with residential sections along them. There were numerous refineries called centrals and distilleries there as well as in Colonial Gardenas area. The north shore of the city was the fishing center.

It was sort of encyclopedic data, but better than no

information. Our job was to discover which refinery was to be the target. Our guess was it had to be of recent vintage and one of Castro's examples of new technology.

"Steve, I do know someone in the town that may help us."

"May?" The tone of questioned excitement was present in my voice as we proceeded along the lovely route of this old town.

"I went to school with him at Penn State. He took engineering and went on to get a Masters in Agricultural Economics. I was never sure where his loyalty was. Was it to Castro or to Cuba. It will be a gamble."

I stopped the cycle and turned my head to see her response. "Do you know where to find him? And, can we get to see him without getting caught?"

"It shouldn't be too bad, although he does live in the town near the old 17th century Palace of Justice. If we act like tourists and go straight there, we may make it. Isn't that what they teach in America, act like you belong and know what you're doing? Simon could be invaluable to us."

"Who is Simon?"

"That's his name."

I adjusted my floppy hat and proceeded into town as if I knew where I was going. Or as close as possible with a rider on the back screaming directions in your ear. We were careful to avoid streets with large or any congregation of police or military.

Joyce's friend worked at a technical school in the city. We hoped he would be home this early. It would be too risky to go to the school and find him

"Which house is it Joyce? Are we near the Old Palace." "I don't know exactly. I'll have to ask."

"OK, I'll just sit here and act inconspicuous on this old noisy cycle", responding in a cynical manner.

"Don't be cute. I don't run around with an alumni roster in my pocket."

While she was locating the house, it was up to me, as far as I could tell, to formulate what to do if Simon Harter decides not to help us and runs to the authorities. Not being a person to like violence, killing him would not be accepted, but putting him out of action would be necessary. Perhaps locking him up in a closet for several days with his mouth gagged. I have always had a fear of that being done to me. With my sinus condition, breathing through my mouth is essential. I would suffocate in no time being gagged and bound.

"This is his place." I jumped straight up not expecting her back so soon. My mind was adrift and she came from the back.

"The large old white one. He must be wealthy...Oh, excuse me, powerful."

"No, he lives on the second floor."

"I've always enjoyed these large old square Spanish homes with the porches off the living room. It looks like there is a porch there on the side that overlooks the yard and street. The woodwork and tile must be beautiful in this place."

"We'll see let's go up."

When we got to the second floor, Joyce began to bang on the door. "Simon. . . Simon are you there? It's me, Joyce. . Joyce Hurtado from Penn State."

I couldn't help but crack a big smile. Joyce from Penn State sounded like a peculiar salutation, especially in the middle of an old Spanish city in Cuba.

There was some shuffling about inside the apartment. And the door opened slowly. I was expecting someone who looked Spanish and intellectual. What I got was something quite different. -Here was this fellow, medium long dark hair, average height and slender, very fair skin, wire rim glasses with a curly perm. He could have been out of the early 1970's dress period.

"Who's he?"

"He is Stephen Masters, a friend of mine. We need help. Will you let us in?"

"Joyce, dear, are you in some trouble?"

"Simon, you aren't aware of what's going on, are you?"

"No, I'm on sort of a vacation. Please come in. But I must warn you, I may not be the best person to be around. I've been critical of some of the agricultural policies and my career is being 'reviewed' at the technical school."

"What? You must be mistaken."

"No, I am not. At a recent meeting of the Agricultural Planning Group, several of us took sharp exception to Fidel's revamped long-range plans. Among the group, I was the most vocal."

"Excuse me, but what is wrong with being an objector? That's how better plans come into being."

"Not in Cuba, Stephen, especially of late. Fidel is the final 'expert' on everything - even what he is not capable of deciding upon. Since then I have been granted a leave while my qualifications are being reviewed. It's sort of a time period for me to think and apologize - at least that's how I see it."

"Simon, Steve and I have to relate to you some information that has happened to us. After which, we are going to need some help from you."

We began to tell the story to Simon beginning with the plane trip and left nothing out. Well, we left a few things out that weren't part of the overall plot but concerned us personally.

"Your tale sounds like it's from a mystery novel. What can I do for you?"

"First, in 200 words or less, describe sugar refineries for a Yankee. That may help figure how they will try and destroy the refinery. Second, why a refinery? Third, which refinery?"

"From the beginning, in 200 words or less. The process begins with cutting ripe cane in about four foot lengths. These are batched and sent to a mill or factory; they are shredded and brushed between huge rollers to extract the juice. This juice is then heated with some lime."

"Why lime?"

"Lime helps impurities to raise and be skimmed off in the scum. The clear juice is boiled and concentrated by evaporation until a mixture of sugar crystals and syrup is reached. Modern factories separate these by centrifugal machines. The crystals become raw or brown sugar, the syrup is molasses. The crushed cane is called bagasse. Generally it was used as fuel in the factory or as fertilizer. Recently it is being utilized to make a building material, like a particle board.

"From this factory, the raw sugar goes to the refinery. It goes in and passes through about seven or eight processes such as affinition, recovery, melting, carbonation, filtration, charring, crystallization, and granulation. With minor changes, the once raw sugar will come out as cubes, fine, maybe your ordinary sugar, or even as coffee crystals in suitable packages. Untouched by humans. In modern times, sugar is one of the purest substances manufactured on a large scale.

"What we called refineries, were old and outdated in many cases. A trend was developing where the factory process was here and the refining elsewhere was outsourced to other countries. For Castro to reach the ultimate goal of 11 million tons of exported sugar a year, a goal that has continually eluded him, more of the process needed to be kept in Cuba to have more growth potential for the Island and her people."

"How is that?"

"Agra development, especially technical agricultural development is the fastest way to satisfy fundamental needs of an impoverished people. If you study Fidel's speeches, this theme is readily present. To do only the factory work leaves us like a colony. We would have to buy our own product back in refined form.

"Fidel has spent much time and money to build some of the super colossal sugar cane-to-refinery to the end product factory centers. They are placed near the sugar fields, but are also close to the sea ports. Matanzas was the location of the newest and largest. It produces all the end products including crystal coffee and icing sugars for sale to communist bloc countries.

"The modern factory is like a shrine of applied agricultural science. The workers are skilled technicians. A tribute to greatness of a leader who can deliver on his promises. To put these out of service would be a major setback in upgrading workers."

"Can you take us to this new refinery?"

"Yes."

"Simon."

"Yes, dear Joyce."

"Is there any way to find where the CIA man or men might be hidden in the Sierra del Rosario Mountains?"

"That will be more difficult. As you know, there are caves and valleys and the like. But it is still close to the capital and there are many people, so the possible sites are less. We can check the more remote areas."

"We have about a day and a half, as I figure it, to be safe."

"That doesn't give us much time to look. We're about an hour from the mountains here. I suggest we go by the refinery and then to the mountains."

"Let's eat and gather what we need."

We hid the cycle in back of Simon's house and headed his vehicle to the refinery. The car was a Ford of the European variety, sort of boxy, but functional. It was a short ride across the edge of the city and out to the refinery. The car was pulled off the road behind some foliage and we began walking across a field. The reason for this eluded me at first. But if one is casing a place, you don't wander up to the front gate and ask to look it over.

As we crawled up the crest of the hill in the field, the refinery complex came into full view. It was huge. Large unloading areas in the center that resembled what the grain elevator areas are at the Pennsylvania grain cooperatives. The initial processing part was to the left and the refinery was center and right. The front right and center of the factory facing the port was the shipping area. There were railroad tracks and conveyors to take the finished goods to a ship or by train or to waiting planes. The three large smokestacks on the left belched dark smoke, while the two stacks in the center were clean. I assumed this had to do with which part of the process was involved.

The complex was enclosed by wire fencing and a main gate. There were other gates, but they were locked, and no traffic was involved.

"I'm no commando, but if I were to try and put this operation out of business, the section where the recovery, melting and carbonation takes place is there. (Pointing to part of the complex in the center). I would destroy that section first, the rest of the refinery next, the factory last. There are many factories. If it is destroyed, the process can still be run by starting with raw sugar at the refinery area."

"The other gates and the fencing don't appear particularly menacing, more to act as a deterrent to entry. We better check to be sure. I wonder about the guards and how many there are?

Let's split up and check all around and get a count of guards, gates, and routes they take. That will help us figure the most logical approach points."

"We should meet back here in no less than two hours if we are to get to the mountains and look around some before dark. It would be nice to know guard change schedules."

"If you can get into or close to the guard but at one of the unmanned gates, the schedules of the workers will be posted. It may provide the information."

"Be careful men."

"What's the purpose behind that comment Joyce? A little feminine machismo?"

"Two hours!" Simon interrupted rather sternly.

I crawled down to get a closer look at my area assignment and count guards. With each movement closer, I had the urge to look quick and hurry back to the meeting point and wait in safety. My stomach was one big

248

acid pit and my heart rate was high. Yet, there was no real danger if one is careful. The movie spies have the assurance of knowing all will go their way. This was no movie set and with my luck, I could end up shot.

Touching the fence to see if it was electric could hurt so a stick was chosen versus my hand. It wasn't. In fact, the locked gate was not particularly secure. A pair of bolt cutters or whatever and entry was easy. This was no top secret compound. Just a new highly technical food processing facility with no reason to be secured tightly. It would be like a plot to blow up the Hershey Chocolate Plant. There are guards at it, but not with the thought in mind they're guarding a top secret operation. Just a big chocolate factory.

Not being an engineer, what the facility did in my area of surveillance remained a mystery. I only hoped to try and figure enough to predict where and how a raid might be staged. From what evidence was present, any time would work. However, evening would be the safest for all parties, including the workers. And, there was less chance of the military being alerted to arrive in sufficient time to stop the mission or arrest the group.

As would be guessed, the other two returned after me. They agreed that an evening raid, after workers and activity had stopped, would be the best. Or in similar fashion, an early morning attack. There were only three guards counted. One at the gate at all times and two on patrol. Hardly a formidable defense against a revolutionary group.

We decided to go look for the CIA man in the mountains. Simon was going to stop by a construction site on the way for supplies. Somehow, our little group resembled the Hardy Boys and Nancy Drew to me. A more formidable group image would be better for my confidence.

"What does Simon want at a construction site?"

"He wants to steal some explosives."

"Oh my."

"Stephen, with the explosives set around the outside of the refinery, we have a better chance against the group. How else are we going to defend the plant? We have two guns with nine bullets between them from the guards in the jeep. How much help will that be for three people against a small platoon of attackers?"

"The more I think about it, the more I feel you're correct Joyce. Let's escape through the south at Guantanamo." "Simon?"

"Yes, dear Joyce, what are your concerns", said in a condensing tone? I can tell by the sound of your voice you have issues or questions."

I interrupted by placing my hands over my face. "My God, a psychic - what do you know about explosives?"

"Enough. I worked on a construction gang doing demolition work, wrecking buildings, before and during college." Simon looked at me and laughed, patted my head and continued. "Steve, there is a concrete factory being constructed just southwest of Habana, near where we are going. We can get wires, explosives and dynamite there. Then we will go look for the CIA man. With some success I hope. However, we are going to have to leave early enough to get back to the refinery in time to ring the perimeter along the most logical access points to the integral refinery functions."

"Where are we going to be during this?"

"We, my American friend, are going to be inside the compound and part way up the refinery with enough height to follow the events of the raid. That is, except for the person who is to set the charge off."

"Simon, it might be better if two of us were below and one above to shoot and direct us where and when to ignite charges."

"There is only one thing for certain - Fidel will never allow any more students to attend Penn State because of you both."

We drove for a few miles to the construction site. "Here we are - I don't see any guards – over there the sheds are near the office site."

"Simon - there are two guard dogs."

"Oh no"

"If they are trained properly, we will have to shoot them for lack of other choices. Or, if they are just big mean dogs, we can get around them by distraction and knock them out."

"What do politicians know of guard dogs?"

"My talents are many, my lady - allow me. Give me the gloves you bought Simon. Joyce, you go up the fence now and throw a series of stones at that dog over there. I will go over the fence with you. You will go behind the large crate. Simon . when this dog has his mouth over my hand, hit him quick - your gloves aren't thick. The next dog will return from the distraction caused by Joyce and we'll do the same. If you don't knock them out, then a hand down the throat will suffocate them."

The dog problem was solved with some pain and a great deal of sweat and fear on my part. The storage shed was locked, but easily opened. Simon knew what to take and he gathered some extra for good measure.

"What the hell is taking him so long?" Asking out loud and to no one in particular.

"He'll be back, he's adjusting something in the storage shed to look inconspicuous at first."

"We've got what we need - let's finish our trip to the mountains gang," Simon pointing to our way out of there.

"Thank God, Simon. It was getting spooky just sitting here."

The trip to the mountains from there was not long, just frightful. I knew everyone suspected us in the car. But there Simon didn't know my fears, and appeared in touch with what was going on.

"Simon."

"Yes, Joyce."

"This plan you're helping us with. Your current career review could be to your benefit. But this action and helping us very well could destroy it. You'll have to leave Cuba."

"I am here in Cuba for love of my country and her people. Not the leaders. If I can't work within the system to help, then other avenues must be found outside the system. Correct? So I help and maybe have to leave Cuba and work in Miami with the anti-Castro groups. I still will help my country."

We parked the car and were about to exit. Joyce offered a search plan that involved spacing ourselves and walking in parallel lines up and down looking for entrances to caves. We had to be quick and if nothing was found, to move back. Our time was short. The whole attempt to save the CIA man was in reality from nervous energy or desperate hope. It would be like combing the mountains at a large State Park in Pennsylvania for the entrance to a limestone cave. Like the ones in central Pennsylvania. Random chance to first pick the correct mountain.

Assuming we could do that, it would still be pure luck to find the entrance. I'm sure the police have searched the area before us. The most important step was not here but was to position ourselves at the refinery to stop the raid.

Chapter 11
THE NETWORK HELPS IT OUT

Robert Jamison, General Penwell and a council aide sat in the car in front of the facility location about to exit, Penwell had just finished giving the aide instructions when. Jamison interrupted.

"General, we must go inside. Call me in an hour."

"Sir?" The aide asked with a slight question in his voice.

"One hour."

"Yes sir." With some reservation, the order was unusual from Robert Jamison. The aide tightened his grip on the wheel and sped quickly up the street to park and return. "Call

me in an hour" was code that
meant something may be wrong.

Jamison entered the bathroom,
cleaned the mirror and placed his
hand over it and began to go to the
closet. The general followed.

"Excuse me General, you forgot
to 'sign in' so to speak.'

"Oh for Christ sake, Robert -
you know me and this is a waste of
time." Robert turned and pushed the
numerical entry code for the day.

It was a simple code that
involved multiplying the days in a
year by the number of the day it was
and dividing by the number of the
month and adding one's personal
entry number.

A star pushed, plus a special
code, warned of something - a person

being followed or being accompanied
by force. Robert pushed the star
button and the emergency code.

The door opened, both men walked
in, the General turned and pointed a
gun at Jamison ordering him past the
receptionist desk and into the
conference chamber.

Robert looked at the General and
smiled.

"You don't seem surprised,
Robert - what the hell is going on?
Or have you been around this cloak
and dagger shit so long your nerves
are dead?"

"No, General - or whoever you
might be. I figured there was a
problem in the car. Aides are never
involved in that type of
conversation. Even if they're my own

personal aide. Not conforming to entry procedures certainly was an easy give away."

"Drop the gun, General -- now." The aide put the pistol behind the General's head.

"He will fire. You should at least know that much." Robert again smiled. Jamison took the General's gun and two other staff aides came out.

"Take him, shoot him up with drugs and find out what the hell is going on here. I want to know soon. If he is uncooperative or we can't get the information - dispose of him."

Jamison went into the conference room. "I assume you heard that interchange outside?"

"Robert, do you think he wanted to infiltrate us because of the Cuban problem?"

"I don't think so. It seems too farfetched."

"Let's press on, shall we", former Undersecretary of State Herd spoke up. "We have been pushing hard on the information network and some troublesome patterns surfaced. We have significant numbers of confrontations forming in second and third world areas. Areas like Angola in Africa, Central America in El Salvador and Honduras, South America in Venezuela and Columbia. But all these are movements that directly or indirectly involve Cuban revolutionary troops or advisors, as they're called."

"Is that the same sort of advisors we have sent to Vietnam and places south?"

"Yes, Admiral."

"Oh, shit, regular troops for combat."

"In some of the areas, such as Central America, the fighting and trouble are involving U.S. backed troops or groups. Other areas, it's a counter-resistance movement. The hell of it is, some of these are Chinese financed troops fighting Cubans. That's plain damned insane."

"Robert, I don't know that these events are connected to our agent in Cuba or any possible problems, but I may have some help for us from an unusual source."

John Greyson, Assistant Director of the CIA, spoke up. His appearances at the group meetings were by necessity rare. Being a member of two clandestine organizations, especially when one is the CIA, is not a safe practice for one's career or health.

"I have arranged a televised interview on our special T.V. cable circuit. The person is at the site in town. He was flown in from Miami early today. As you know, he can't hear our voice or see us, all our questions are relayed through the aide at the program site. But, we have visual and audio of the source."

"I'll turn it on for you, John. Let's get this program in gear. We need more information."

"Okay, gentlemen, our subject is Carlo Romeo from Cuba. He is mid-forties, well educated, speaks fluent English among other languages. He is a field worker, and a member of a very special anti-Castro underground."

"John - a well-educated middle aged field worker? Is this a joke?"

"If you have trouble, Admiral, with this much information about him, the rest is going to be very difficult for you. Shall I proceed?"

"Yes, John."

"Thank you, Robert - Mr. Romeo and his cohorts are homosexuals."

"Damn queers!"

"Admiral, please bear with me." John looked around the room. Herd indicated he wished to speak. "Yes, Mr. Herd."

"Our CIA sources will definitely substantiate the homosexual group as a discriminated body in Cuba. We don't, however, have any record of their being an organized resistance movement. Although there was talk of trying to organize them, very hush-hush."

"Let me continue. The monolithic collectivism practiced by the Socialistic government is most effective in elevating the life standards of women and blacks in Cuba. The equality and growth of making everyone equal and the same is quite effective. Yet, it is equally effective in reverse discrimination against homosexuals."

"The result is that this group with its particular inclinations are deprived of good jobs, companionship and rights granted to heterosexuals in the country."

Robert peered up, his hands held in prayer fashion under his chin, smiled and asked, "How can this fellow be of any help to us, John?"

"He has some information about our duo that could be helpful and they, Romeo's group, are sympathetic and in need of friends."

"Which means a base of support for our operatives in Cuba."

"Correct, Mr. Herd."

"I don't like queers!" The Admiral leaned back in his chair, lit a cigar and folded his arms across his chest.

"Excuse me gentlemen - let's hear the data." Robert spoke up before an argument could begin and looked at John, nodded his head and continued, "Have Mr. Romeo explain to us what he has learned about Stephen Masters and Joyce Hurtado."

"My name is Carlo Romeo. I and others in similar circumstances are being treated very poorly by the Castro government. They are a narrow minded group who will not allow us. to pursue our own life style."

"Your political friend from Pennsylvania and Joyce have escaped from the political revolutionaries headed by Dante Perez. The word put out is that Joyce freely went over to the rebel group and the American is a CIA plant to foster insurrection."

"Surely, the government would not believe such stories?"

"Don't be too certain," stated Romeo. "They have issued warrants for their arrest and attempted an arrest already. Besides, don't you have a CIA man named Arthur Harrington in Cuba now?"

"My God, how do you know that?" asked Greyson. "That's classified information. I know he's there, but not what his mission is. It's top drawer, need-to-know-only."

Carlo continued. "He was sent to talk to pro-American groups of supporters. We are such a group. Unfortunately, he didn't find his way to us or he would not be captured."

"The Castro government hasn't reported his capture. They would not miss such an opportunity for propaganda."

"He was captured by the Perez group", Carlo answered Greyson's remark. "For what purpose, we don't know. Maybe that is where the American and the girl are wandering."

"Wandering - ask what the hell he means by that?"

"They were held prisoner on the eastern mountain area, Mr. Greyson. To escape quickly and with more ease would be to go south to Guantanamo. Yet their movement has been toward Habana by crossing the remote districts to get there. As if they were looking for someone. They have taken days to complete what otherwise would be an eleven hour drive down the main central highway across Cuba."

"That damn Masters thinks he's campaigning for office in Cuba!' The Admiral banged his head with his hand. "All them damn politicians have head problems. Ask him if he's been following them. Why didn't he help them?"

"Not following the two. I get reports of their movements by our people and other groups. Also, by government bulletins. Besides, why should we help if you're not going to be helpful to us. It would be risking our lives to expose our identities. Gay liberation is not an openly debated idea in Cuba."

"What do you want from us?" asked Jamison.

"For those who take the persecution, we need a way out - somewhere to go. For those of us who stay money. But even more, certain goodies we can't buy in Cuba."

"Good God", stated Herd. "Whatever happened to revolutionary groups wanting guns and ammunition? Now we supply sheets and erotic sexual paraphernalia."

As I see it, gentlemen, our alliance with this group will serve our purpose. The CIA, I don't believe, would form a permanent alliance with them - is that correct, Mr.Greyson?"

"Robert, we probably would not, they would be considered too unstable."

"Let's see what we can arrange. Ask him, or tell him we will cooperate."

"Robert."

"Yes, Admiral."

"Do we ask more agents to return to Cuba, or do we limit exposure by just helping this group to get them out? Personally, I'm in favor of limited exposure. We don't know the extent of our problems in Cuba, or what these international situations will amount to."

"How do the rest of you feel?"

"Herd?"

"I agree with the Admiral."

"So do I, Robert."

"I do, as well, which makes it a majority vote. Make the argroup, along with some conventional materials." Robert indicated to shut off the video display. "Gentlemen, it's time for us to go. We all have our jobs to complete. I will be in Miami, Key Biscayne, to be precise this coming week. There is a rather important conference to take place and I want to be available to help our not so smooth politicians. You know the codes and locations to contact me. We'll use Miami as a base to follow the escape of our dynamic duo."

Chapter 12
IT'S DARK AND WET

"I'm sorry you're involved in this mess. You're not even CIA."

Arthur Harrington, the longtime service CIA man looked at Frank Bush and Eric Johnson, both military intelligence officers. Both were weak, but Eric was dying from the punishment by the Perez group during questioning. Arthur couldn't believe the size of the cavern in this part of the cave. It was a large room, but apparently not as large as some others where he could hear voices of many others speaking.

The glow of the lantern cast crazy shadows with the rock formations in the cave. To keep his courage up, and to take his mind off how tired, cold and hungry he was,

277

he would try to imagine what different shapes the shadows made. Sort of like when he was a kid making a game out of formations from clouds.

It was hard to imagine how the military didn't know of this place so close to Havana. Yet, his knowledge of the current state in Cuba answered that. Castro had successfully broken up most of the bandit group's years before. There wasn't the need for as tight of control as before in this area. The remote regions were depopulated first, then reorganized carefully to discourage the reappearance of the bandit groups. The apparent confidence of the government left enough looseness of contact to some clever groups like this one and a few others to operate.

"Relax, Arthur, no one ever said military intelligence would be a nine-to-five job with no risks. I'm not feeling well, but my cohort Eric is bad off."

"Oh hell, I liked Eric Johnson. Damn, Frank, we have to be able to get out of here. We've been in tough spots before."

"Arthur, this looks bad for the visiting team. I've lost all track of time in this cave. We've not eaten and Johnson and I have been beaten rather badly. These aren't ropes on us, they're chains and I can't see very well by the light of one small lantern."

"Who is the Cuban fellow they brought in before?"

"Was that last night, or last morning - and this is now night?"

"I think it was morning."

"I don't know. He's a major by the uniform insignia. I think he's drugged, or a damn sound sleeper."

Drugged I believe, Frank. I didn't realize you two were here for a day and a half. You both were out like a couple of stones." "There must be something going on or soon to be in the works. There have been a good number of people from the Perez group in and out of here in the last hours."

"If your intuition is like mine, we will fit into this flurry of activity."

"Frank, do you remember what I told you about the conversations I overheard?"

"If those are pieced together with the chatter today - - I think you're correct. I hate to say so, but your intuition may be on target."

"They still don't believe Eric Johnson and I aren't CIA. Damn near beat him to death over it. See what you think of this idea, Arthur."

Frank adjusted himself as well as possible from his chained position to relay a plan to escape. The plan was more hope than anything else. But it was better than giving up and dying. It was your basic plan where they create a decoy by attracting attention then jump the person from the back. Used everywhere from T.V. shows to street muggers. It was as good as he could handle now.

Dante stood up to get the attention of the man. They were excited about the upcoming assault on the refinery.

"Hey! Quiet. . Listen to me now. We proceed with the sugar refinery tomorrow night after dark. They aren't running the facility full time around the clock. There are only a few things that must be kept running. That means only a few, maybe two or three, technicians plus the guards will be there."

"We want to approach from the field."

"Why not the other side?"

"Because it is all finished product processes, putting it into boxes and the like and shipping. If we blow that up, they slip out the side door for Christ sake. The same with the factory processing area. If we knock it out another will be used around the clock and the semi-processed goods shipped in. We have enough men and fire power to take out the refinery part completely. The fire should spread quickly to the other sections. I don't want my troops dying or wasting effort anywhere else."

"Perez Guerra is the main assault leader to blow up the refinery. We've told you who will be with him."

"Juan is leading the group who will portion the CIA man and his accomplices and be the first attack group to try and take out

The guards"

"Perez"

"Si Dante. . . .we want to be ready to move in quickly. Juan and his groups' main objective is to place the CIA man and take out the main gate guard. And then cover our advance to set the charges."

"While he is talking, has anyone checked our guest recently?"
"About an hour ago Dante. You mean the Americans and Fidel's man?"

"Yes, not the man from the train who lost Masters and the girl. We will take care of him shortly. Send some people to be sure they are not doing anything. I will explain the escape plans after Perez is finished. Juan, go take care of the idiot from the train, who can't beat up a woman. Take the girl. She is a good protégé for you, no?"

"Ha, ha, yes, she swings a mean machete. I am glad she made it here from the other end of the island."

-------- --------------------

"Frank."

"Yes, Arthur"

"Do you really believe this idea has a chance?"

"No, but I can't think of anything better, and I don't feel like dying in a damn cave in Cuba."

Eric Johnson and the Cuban officer were placed in a sitting

position clearly visible upon entry into the room where they were held captive.

Arthur and Frank, hands chained in front, were on either side of the entry way to the room. They had removed the belts from the other men and themselves to be used as weapons. Plus, Arthur had a stone big enough to knock a man out. The plan was crude for men of cloak and dagger persuasion.. .Let the first person in a few feet, take him out with the rock and choke the next with a belt. The problems start if there are three people in the group.

"What if no one comes for a couple of hours? I'll get a cramp in this position Frank."

"They'll be here. They check every hour or so it seems."

"I wish they'd hurry. I'm getting tired and weak."

"Here comes someone!"

The entrance to the room was about four feet seven inches high, forcing the average size person to duck down. This offered the weakened duo a slight advantage. As luck would have it, there were only two men. The first ducked and entered, walked two steps slightly crouched. The scenario was perfect for him and Arthur's rock proved sufficient to the task. The next man was behind him. Frank started to choke from the back and the strong revolutionary ran his elbow into Frank's stomach. Arthur had to use the stone, but not before receiving a kick in the chest. With all his strength, Frank pulled him back, and Arthur slammed the stone into the face of the Cuban.

The blood began to flow from the broken blood vessels in the forehead, and the Cuban slumped to the ground. The two grabbed their weapons and headed out the entrance.

"Don't you think it would be wise if we could have propped them near Eric and the army guy, to make it look like 'we were all still there?"

"Yes, but we don't have much time, I feel."

Frank and Arthur headed out the low passageway and fumbled along the dark corridor as quietly as possible, until they came to a fork in the corridor with two options.

"Oh, shit, a selection of passageways."

"Let's go this way" Arthur whispered.

"Why?"

"Perhaps you know the way Frank?" Arthur mused in a cynical fashion.

"Ok, OK"

The two desperate and tired men moved down the narrow‾, wet passageways as quietly as possible, crouched and trying to use the flashlight sparingly. Another corridor connected into theirs from the left and they continued straight ahead about twenty feet straight from where the last corridor joined.

They entered another room. A man was tied up and unconscious on the ground.

"Who the hell is that?"

Arthur stared "Looks like a bum, sort of like the others."

"This isn't our day, I hear someone coming."

They raced for what looked like a way out, but was only a closet-like room off the main room. Both men went flat on the floor and hid off to the side of the entrance way.

"What is this shit we're laying in Arthur?"

"Judging by the color, and its independent movement, I'd say it's about three inches of bat shit."

"That's alive with bacteria!"

"If we live, I'll personally clean your body with Lysol. Now shut up Frank."

Into the room came Juan and a stern-looking revolutionary girl. What followed could only be considered a bizarre and sick show of death and sex.

They awakened the tied Cuban fellow and began to slap and kick him. Asking him why he let the American and the girl go. They screamed that he should have died on the train as his comrades died.

Frank and Arthur seemed confused. What American and what girl? Who the hell was out there?

The girl took out her knife and cut open the man's trousers and began a sadistic torture of the prisoner. She was taking the knife in light strokes across his testicles. The man was gagged, but the muffled screams were deafening. His face was scarlet with pain and the blood vessels stood out like small ropes as he yelled.

The psychological transformation of the sadistic duo was more than Frank and Arthur had ever witnessed. It resembled a frenzy similar to that of sharks. Only the couple was finding the acts sensual. The knife strokes on the penis were deep and the prisoner was bleeding to death and screaming.

Then the unbelievable began to happen. Juan and the girl began to embrace and claw at each other. They began to make love while this man was screaming and bleeding to death.

It was a wild sexual act resembling two mad dogs and in their similar position so they both could watch the prisoner.

The only mercy was his death. Frank was about to throw up. He held on hoping the couple would leave. When they left, carrying the lantern, Frank crawled out to the man. Arthur sat beside him and cried.

"My God, I've seen a lot in this job, but this, this is more than I can handle."

"Let's get the hell out of here."

The two went out of the room and took the corridor they passed earlier. Its outcome was at another fork in the cave, only this time the

293

choice was more evident. Noise could be heard to the left. They went right and headed till the tunnel came to an opening. At the opening was a patrol sitting with his back to the opening of the cave. 'Revenge, hate, and sickness all pent up from the vile display took its toll. The two jumped the guard and killed him with swift dispatch.

"Where do we go Arthur?"

"Down the mountain. I can find our way soon. There are a lot of houses and people all through this area. There are some popular for their caverns and that sort of shit."

"How do they go undetected?"

"Well, as near as I can figure", Arthur talked as they walked. .

."It's because there is no road near this area. We have to go over another small mountain after we cross this narrow valley."

The valley was about three hundred yards followed by another mountain.

"When do we get these chains off Art?"

"As soon as it's safe to use a gun to shoot them off. I'd say over the rim of the next mountain. By then they will discover we are gone and be after us."

"What do you mean, two of the prisoners are gone" Dante. screamed.

"When the guards did not return, I went to check. This man here, who was sent to check on them, was knocked out, the other dead."

Dante turned and gave stern orders. "Take a small group and look. They haven't eaten in days. They will be weak. I want them back."

"Juan!"

"Take this idiot to the train prisoner. You know how to teach him not to make stupid mistakes."

"Oh, ha ha. . .yes I do."

Perez asked about the necessity to have the two for the success of the plan. Dante replied that they still had one CIA man and the Cuban officer. It would still work.

"When do you think we should leave? I mean - do we wait till they have been returned?"

"No Perez, we go as planned. There are too many errors already. Any delays could only mean more chance of another stupid mistake."

Chapter 13
MUCH TO OUR SURPRISE

"Simon, there are a lot of people living in this area. Don't you think this idea of a revolutionary hide-out is a bit offbeat?"

Simon looked at me with a stern stare then spoke. "We walk over this mountain to the next. There is no road to it. If they are here, it will be along that mountain or its valley area. See, it's not as bad as you thought, Steve."

The whole idea including Simon was not making any sense to Steve. Jesus, there are a lot of caves in Pennsylvania. There are limestone formations. Not as many as the Western Virginia area, but enough.

I used to explore as a kid. They were hard to find then, and I knew what I was looking for and basically where they were.

Another thing bothered me. Why was Simon so helpful? I heard his patriotic explanation. But it didn't fit. Neither did it fit that a teacher would be as good with tools of terrorists as he seemed to be. What was worse, the guy just didn't seem the part. How many refined revolutionaries do you find! He didn't even spend much time or interest in Joyce's body. I guess I shouldn't judge another's behavior by my own patterns. Hell, I watch her and have fantasies even during tense moments. The walking will do me Good.

"Steve, what are you thinking about? You seem in deep thought."

"Don't ask, Joyce, you'll only think I'm a pervert,"

"Oh hell, you can't be that passionate - you're not even Latin."

"Okay, I'm admiring the flora and fauna of this shitten mountain. No, -- I'm sorry. I'm interested in getting back to the refinery. I think that's the place to be."

"Well, I think you're right. But we must try."

"I know - - -it was sort of a necessary extension of our journey."

We hid our car with some brush and branches, enough to be overlooked by casual passing of the area. From this, we started toward the area where Simon thought the CIA agent might be held prisoner.

As a fellow from Pennsylvania, used to seeing tropical plants in my house in little pots, tripping over giant replicas seemed too much to accept. I had this unexplainable compulsion to rip some up to take home with me.

We had made it over the crest of the first mountain. Well, let's put these mountains into perspective. They're about as high as the Appalachian range in Pennsylvania, Maryland and Virginia. No overwhelming job to climb around, 800 - 1000 feet I would guess was the elevation of this one and not a steep grade. Just enough to be modestly sweaty and tired from walking uphill for a long time. Just over the crest Simon noticed some activity about a quarter of a mile away.

It looked like some men running or attempting to run. That is not an astounding revelation except for the way they were running. It looked like their arms were stuck out in front of them. Not the normal movement of alternating alongside of the body. Joyce pointed out that it could be that their hands were tied and they could be escaped prisoners, perhaps the CIA man.

"Steve, do you recognize either of them?"-

"Joyce, they are a quarter of a mile away and moving. Besides, I never met the man."

Simon turned and chimed in, "Isn't he from America and in government service, like you?"

"Simon, I am a politician from Pennsylvania. How in the hell would I know a CIA man from God knows where? Jesus, Joyce, give him some idea of how many government employees there are in the U.S."

"Simon, just about one in every six working persons in America is in some form of government service."

"No wonder your country seems confused,"

"Simon, can we go after them and hold the damn labor economics lecture?"

We started in pursuit of the two men. I silently swore to myself that, God forbid, I ever get in another situation like this, I'll jump out of the plane and take my chances at flying before going on one of these crazy expeditions. Here we are running through a mass of shrubs after two people that we aren't sure of, but believe may be, at least one of them, a CIA man. God was I confused.

I still think we overreacted days ago with the two Cuban soldiers. If we had gone with them maybe we could have explained everything and all would be well that ends well. Instead, we attacked them, took their money and guns, and are responsible for two deaths on a train, among other things. That alternative was now closed. So I ran faster and began to figure out what to do when we caught up with these people.

When we got to the vicinity of where an intercept would have been made, they weren't there. I. felt a sharp blow in the back and went head first into a mass of crotons, which prompted a mass of four letter invectives.

"Hey, are you the Americans?"

"And you're a damn genius, who I might guess to be our CIA man."

"Yeah, Arthur Harrington. This is Frank Bush, Military Intelligence."

I looked around and didn't see anyone else. Arthur spoke up. "Behind you, ready to choke you till the swear words come out."

"That's gratitude. This gentlemen is Simon Hortez and the lady is Joyce Hurtado. We have been looking everywhere for you!" slowly stood up and dusted off.

"Well, the amenities must wait. There are some mean people not far behind us."

Those words hardly left Harrington's lips when all hell broke loose. Broke loose with an act of violence so horrible to witness that my entire body was stunned. Frank Bush, whose hand I was yet to shake and greet, fell on his knees with his head split down the middle. I had never seen the insides of a human skull fall out and down the front of a person before. An axe split the head open into two sections. Much as if one would cut a coconut in half. My God the blood, brains, and eyes. Even the mucous from the sinus cavity was splattered about.

Simon began to shoot and Joyce kicked me out of the way to avoid being shot. I fell and tried to catch my senses. But it didn't matter. I vomited my guts up. Arthur, with his hands chained in front of him, was trying to help me keep from getting killed.

Fortunately, there were only three of them. Simon shot two and Joyce tripped one in front of Arthur, who then strangled him with the chain on his wrists.

There was no time to lose. Joyce shot the lock on Arthur's chains and we had to run. The gun shots would not only attract the attention of Dante's men, who I must assume these three represented, but it may also bring the authorities.

At least Frank's body would be unrecognizable and could not be used in any scheme.

I had to stop. I vomited two more times till we made it back to the car. Joyce was rubbing my back. She didn't have the front row seat to see the killing of Frank like I did. Her system was still intact.

At the car, Joyce and I piled in the back and Simon and Art embraced like old friends before getting into the car and driving. "You two know each other?" I asked.

Harrington spoke out. "We'll bring you up on that soon, Masters.

You said you had a tale to tell me. Let's hear it."

We gave a quick summary of the end result at the sugar refinery to give our ultimate point to the story. Then started back with the airline ride and the hijacking. We gave every detail about it and our stay in the mountains and the trip to get to this point, with a few personal items excluded, but not leaving out the witch doctor routine and the bums on the train. With the story leading up to our current encounter.

We were heading the car in the general vicinity of Simon's apartment. Harrington needed some food and clothes. Rest would also help, but that probably wouldn't be in the schedule. Joyce and I were anxious to hear his story now, but he fell asleep after a few comments back to us.

Inside Simon's apartment, we grabbed a quick bite of food and some clothes. Arthur Harrington began to relate the saga in the cave and a wild story about the sexual rite.

"Joyce, how would I send a note to the cycle owner to be sure he gets it back?"

Simon echoed in, "I'll do that, Steve."

"Arthur, why are you in Cuba? It wasn't revealed in your story why you are here or why Frank and Eric were here? What the hell's going on?"

"It's rather a difficult answer, one that I'm not sure you will want to hear."

"What do you mean not want to hear?"

"I don't know for sure why Johnson was here. The best I can tell, it had to do with checking arms shipments to Central American countries to support guerilla activities there."

Joyce smiled. She couldn't resist saying something. "The Americans have always been here in one way or another Steve. They think of Cuba as a joining property with right of access."

"Well put Joyce." Simon smiled.

"Thank you Simon."

"Oh, shit, can we hear the answer?" I couldn't believe the political banter at a time like this.

"I'm top drawer secret file experiment of the CIA" Arthur started.

"Experiment?" My forehead ruffled.

"We need support in Cuba. There is a good deal of unrest in our hemisphere emanating from this island,. CIA felt it was time to create a few 'activities', if you will, to keep the Castro government concentrating on their own home front."

I answered, "That's no secret: Every eighth grade world cultures student knows that."

"They don't know this plan. I doubt even the brass in the Pentagon have been briefed on this one."

"What makes you so unusual?" I snapped, growing impatient with this round-about explanation.

"Will you let him finish, Steve?" Joyce said.

OK"

Art began again, "I'm a homosexual CIA agent, sent to infiltrate this group in Cuba and gain support for gathering information and creating what we call activity, or as you refer to as trouble, for the Castro government."

I began to chuckle and shake my head. It did seem like a CIA plan and it didn't. Most of the CIA people I've met were macho types.

But the thinking to come up with this fit their level of intellect.

Arthur looked at me in a very serious manner. "Don't laugh Steve. They are as their American counterparts, well-educated. More so than average.. Plus, many are in high places in government. Those that haven't been found out."

"I'm sorry. It is just hard to picture a group of 'fellows' as hero role models carrying on guerilla activities."

"Nontraditional, yes, but effective" Simon chimed in. I looked over at Simon, "How do you know?"

"I'm part of the homosexual group."

"Simon, you?" Joyce's mouth dropped open.

"What's the matter, Joyce? You didn't have an affair with him in the past, did you?" The thought brought out some more of a chuckle from me.

"Don't be crude Steve. Besides, he did rather well in helping us today."

She had a good point. Although I suspected there was something different about him. "OK, the losing of your job was because you were found out?"

"Very good, Steve. Now, instead of working behind the scene, I will work in a more traditional revolutionary pattern. Or go to the U.S. and help supply support from that group."

"What group?" 'I looked up again puzzled by the answer.

"Castro sent a group of undesirables, as he called them, to America." Simon began to explain. "Many were outright criminals, but many were jailed homosexuals from various job categories who had been found out and began to cause trouble. Only they were without proper direction."

Arthur chimed in, "That's when we became involved. During our interrogation of this group, a trend was spotted. An unusually large group of homosexuals were among those set free to America."

"I don't remember reading about this."

"Of course not Steve. It was kept under wraps. We had a hell of a time with the civil liberties groups for keeping them in custody around the country without due process. But we had to figure this out first."

Arthur continued his explanation. At times, his description of jail scenes and interrogations by macho CIA agents made us all laugh.

The whole idea seemed unbelievable. Yet, the whole action by Castro seemed strange then for some‾reason. Why release a potential group of politically subversive individuals who could return to cause trouble? Unless, you didn't fear or respect them as a real threat. The treatment of homosexuals as described by Arthur and Simon indicated this lack of respect. Could this be Castro's first real strategic mistake?

Simon and Arthur began discussing where they could find some help for our caper at the refinery. Time was now growing short. Joyce and I walked into the kitchen area of Simon's small apartment. We both stared at each other with a half-smile. The message was nonverbal, but clear. What an amusing foursome to try and stop an incident. Two political types who were lovers, and two homosexuals - one a spy and the other a Cuban outcast.

"What do we do now, Steve?"

"Well, my dear, we do a little brainstorming amongst our group and then head out. After all, Arthur is still CIA. Maybe not the average stereotype, but highly thought of to come here to start a base of support.

We walked back into the room with Simon and Arthur and began to formulate some strategy. Simon had some ideas from our earlier reconnaissance. And, he took some demolition supplies from the construction site a few hours earlier while I entertained the dogs.

Joyce drew a map of the refinery for Arthur and gave an indication of what we knew about the rounds of the guards.

The plan we needed was not to try and defeat a larger, better equipped, and trained group. But to be enough of a problem to get them to stop the attempt of destruction. That is, if we could be enough of a bother and make enough noise to stop their attempt.

Chapter 14
TO DEFEND IT

I sat with blind fear in the field awaiting the signal for my initial part of the action. The trip to the refinery was for the most part uneventful. Mostly convoluted discussions of how this hybrid group was put together. I had a good idea but did not chime in in order not to keep my "other life" private. It would have been great to be a "fly-on-the-wall" listening to this discussion and the Admirals comments.

These kind of arrangements to defend this or that against a foe always get me nervous. Especially tonight because I can't see well in the dark and would be running for my life after igniting a massive brush fire in the field outside the fence of the refinery.

The signal from Joyce would tell me that Dante's group was poised for attack. She was up high on a walkway. Our last line of defense and in charge of tossing Molotov cocktails if the assault team made it that far.

Simon was dressed as a guard to create the impression all was normal at the refinery. We were able to subdue the guards and keep them with Joyce. Actually, Arthur did the work. I tied them up. The idea of keeping them near Joyce was for them to see the assault and realize we were the good guys, and hoping then they would be some help upon this realization. Help will be needed. Dante's team of men and women could

be ruthless. I felt rather certain
we all would die in the end. The
plans sounded good on paper in
Simon's apartment and when
discussing it in the car coming
here. Reality is different. None of
us could die too soon for our part
of this defense of the refinery to
be a success. There were no reserve
troops or contingent plans. Just the
fearsome foursome.

I had made the brush piles as
soon as possible after we arrived.
The dry grass and twigs' were
plentiful. It would burn quickly and
the hope was it would rapidly spread
along the fence line. The trick in
making the piles was not to be
obvious about them yet be big enough
to do the job. Hence I went for
elongated thick piles that were tall

grass height that would seemingly blend in with the field.

It would not win a Boy Scout merit badge but would do what we needed for the defense of the refinery.

Joyce gave her signal which for lack of supplies looked like something a ten year old would have devised. She had spotted the assault group. A red light signal that was made via a flashlight through a red jar. Hoping, of course, not to look like a warning signal. My stomach was jumping and I burped from acid churning. Thank God no one was around to hear. I strained my eyes. Yes, I finally saw them crawling along the ground toward the fence.

The brush pile in front of me was soaked in some chemical from the refinery that Simon swore would burn like crazy. Just about to light the pile when a movement was heard behind me. About three feet away was one of Dante's men crawling toward the refinery fence. I had only a piece of pipe for a weapon. Not suspecting me to be hiding, I caught him in the face full force with the pipe. The crunch of flesh and bones was the only sound. He died that fast. My physical body systems were hyped and my strength was more than I figured. He had a pistol. I took it and then lit the brush. Simon wasn't kidding, it jumped into flame like a charcoal fire in a grill soaked with fluid when you first throw a match to the wet coals. I took off running in a half crouched position toward the second pile.

It all sounds so easy when planning. But this was a simple field and not a perfectly smooth soccer playing area. As I ran I kept stumbling in holes in the grass. I moved with all the energy one could muster. But the last days were hardly a best practices training regimen. Combine that with irregular sleep patterns and it was the best running I could muster.

The next pile just did not seem to get any closer despite my efforts. Plus the vision of the person I just killed was in my mental vision. No amount of training or rationalization can make that as matter of fact as is depicted in the movies.

It suddenly dawned on me that if one of Dante's soldiers were in this field there must be others. I had to clear my mind and focus in this moment better. Keep the fatigue and the vision of the dead soldier for another time. Being careless would potentially mean my own death as well. As a team were too thin so that if I failed the mission would be put into jeopardy.

The theory of a couple of brush fires spaced apart was twofold. First, to attract attention from the surrounding area and hope some help would come for us. All of which may cause Dante's group to abandon the idea of destruction at that point. Second, to provide some light for us to see where they were in the field.

The only trouble with the second part is that I could be seen more easily by them.

As I ran to the pile, a shot hit the dust rather close. Side stepping to act evasive and make myself a more difficult target seemed the natural course of action. My first zig went fine, it was the zag that got me. A bullet grazed my right leg.

Lying there in the dirt and grass, I told myself not to panic. Everyone gets a flesh wound on T.V. and the movies. They continue to fight, run and survive just fine. Why then was there so much pain, with an intense desire to cry or pass out?

Confusion was just at a mild stage for the assault team. I could sense this by the chatter and movement noise. Crawling toward the second pile another shot came close and forced me to spin around on my stomach, pistol ready to shoot. I looked. Oh hell, why me, a person with Pennsylvania values to be faced with shooting at a woman revolutionary. Thank God her aim was off. Not be cause of being a woman. Most people can't hit a closet door at 50 feet with a high caliber pistol.

It was a long time since my being on the high school rifle and pistol team, but I fired and hit her in the arm. Good enough to send her to the ground and allow me to get away toward the pile of brush. No

time could be lost. I lit it and
took off limping toward the fence to
help Simon at the gate; which was my
other assignment. The plan was for
Simon to set off the explosives he
stole just outside the fence thirty
seconds after the second brush pile
was set on fire. That was, in
theory, enough time for me to get
away from them and not be blown up
by our own explosives. That was
before I got shot.

No one figured that type of
contingency.

"You've been shot!" he yelled.

"Damn good observation, Simon."
I was sitting, half hidden in the
guard shack and holding my leg.

The explosives were sending dirt
and grass everywhere. I had just

made it to him when they were going off.

"Where is Arthur?"

"He opted for plan B for himself."

Plan B for Arthur Harrington was to be sort of buried below the surface of the ground and wait till the assault group went by him and then to create more confusion by shooting and attacking them from the rear. This, in theory again, would create an illusion of being surrounded and cause the group to abandon the plan. With Arthur's luck the leader, Dante, would probably be standing on his back. We only hoped he could surface and be of some help. Arthur's efforts will trigger a re-think of him and his group's bravery.

The guard shack was under heavy fire and we figured we must get out of it and fall back. The bullets were ripping through the thin wood frame structure and broken glass was everywhere.

"Let's go, Simon, for Christ's sake."

"Okay, now!" he yelled to me.

As he went out the door the lunatic, Juan, kicked open the gate to the refinery. Simon fired and hit him but then his weapon jammed. I couldn't believe my eyes for what happened next. Simon took out the knife he carried and attacked the man, cutting his throat like a pirate of old would have done. I scooted out and attempted to cover for him. We started to back up toward a barricade of empty oil drums. I fell on my ass behind them and as I did, a long blast of bullets came from a machine gun. Simon was hit by the bulk of them and it sent his body crashing back through the barrels and coming to rest several feet behind the drums.

Joyce shot from above or I would have been next take the same treatment as Simon. For a second, I stroked his hair and mumbled something like God save him for heaven. Simon was more man than many I had known in my life. Not just for this scene, but as a person. I flew, with what speed I could muster, to get up the walkway and help Joyce from there. Where the hell was Arthur's diversion?

"Are you okay, Steve?"

"No, I told you this was an insane plan. I got shot in the leg and Simon is dead."

Joyce tossed the first bottled explosive. The scene was unbelievable from up here. It was reminiscent of a grandiose movie set with fires, bombs exploding, and bullets going everywhere, Arthur's plan worried me as we tossed our supply of bottled Molotov cocktail bombs out at the attackers. The fire from the brush had spread and would not allow as easy a retreat for the assault team, especially with him back there shooting. They would have nowhere to go but towards, us.

Joyce cut the guards loose. They looked scared to death and acted such. They ran down the walkway steps toward the back of the refinery. One was shot and killed halfway down and the other was shot by his second step after hitting the ground. So much for their help. Ok, it is a scary situation and the guards do not know who we are. It did probably look strange with an American and a Cuban fighting against Cubans, who themselves were Cubans trying to damage the refinery. So to forgive is divine. But two more defenders would have been really nice.

The darkness confused things and while we had light from a brush fire there were still dark places and uneven lighting. Nor did we count upon the smoke providing cover for their advance.

We needed the explosives real bad. A foursome may work in golf but to defend an entire refinery is greatly overstated optimism. Everything had to go our way.

The first explosive came. It sent two of the assault team flying in the air. Arthur had begun his one man show. Thank God. We had just tossed the last of our bombs and were down to pistols to defend ourselves. A loud shrill whistle sounded. The assault team was no longer shooting, but was in some other maneuver. The first desire was to spot Dante and shoot him. Eliminating him would seriously hinder the hopes of El Movemiento Nuevo Politica. Thanks to the light

from the brush fire we saw Arthur.
He sent another stick of dynamite
toward the direction of the whistle.
It exploded and a scream of pain
could be heard about the noise. The
assault team was leaving. This idiot
refinery would be saved to produce
sugar for the coffee cups of
communists everywhere.

My chest didn't swell in pride.
Only my wounded leg throbbed in
pain.

We went down the stairs to meet
Arthur. The sweat was running down
and smearing the dirt in the black
grease we had put on our faces to be
less noticeable. Joyce had her arm
around me to help me walk.

"We must get out of here
quickly".

We'll be heroes!"

"Damn politicians, always looking for some free press. No, you won't be. Help me drag Simon out of here. We'll all be shot for being a part to this."

"Where do we go Arthur?" Joyce asked.

"Toward the dock. We should be getting some help."

"Why didn't they come sooner?"

"The call Simon and I made before we left the apartment was to secure some help from a group of Simon's friends. They weren't sure how quickly they could get here."

We moved to the docks carrying Simon's body, or what was left of it. We could see vehicles on the road approaching from the distance.

We laid the body down and looked out to the water. Two boats were coming. The motors were turned off as they approached.

"Steve, you and Joyce go in that boat. I must take Simon's body with me and go. They will help you get back to the U.S."

"Where are you going, Arthur?" I yelled.

"I'm here on assignment, Steve. I still have more to do. Besides, if what you told me is correct, you must be sure they don't try their plan in Miami to disrupt the conference."

"I don't think that's a problem now, Arthur, but it's better to be safe."

Arthur took off in the other boat with Simon's body to deliver it to friends who would be sure it would be safe and not used in some propaganda campaign by the government.

His journey while relatively short in time was still fraught with potential issues. The ground were being filled with soldiers and well light from the refinery lights. The soldiers would have high speed boats which could potentially overtake Arthur. Arthur is a long tenure agent who has been in tight spots before. He was wise enough to leave without using running lights on the boat.

About a fifteen minute ride along the shore they ducked into a small inlet and met some of the other members of Simon's group. They were noticeably upset with his death. With care they took him to a waiting old panel truck and placed the body in the back and quickly left. It would not be long before the police and troops would be searching this area. Arthur also had more to do to insure Steve and Joyce actually got away safely. This plan had a lot of assumptions and what if's to get them to the rendezvous point where a helicopter would take them on.

"Joyce, come on now, we have to leave." I felt bad for Joyce. She was trying to brush the hair from Simon's face and had a few tears on her cheek.

"I always thought of him as a gentle and kind person. It's so horrible to see him like this."

"I know. He took the bullets that were aimed for me. They'll take him and be sure he receives the proper funeral, a funeral of a hero."

"It's so stupid. He died helping a government that made him an outcast. He didn't have to be a part of this. He did it for us, you know."

We were in the boat and pulling away quickly. The whole area near the front of the refinery was filling with soldiers or police.

"Joyce, none of this made sense. If we had been able to go to the authorities and explain our case, the whole adventure of getting here could have been avoided. But, it wasn't that way." I went on as if talking to myself. "If for no other reason than to prevent a useless destruction of property our action was correct. Political theories aside, there comes a time when this sort of terrorism cannot be tolerated. The innocent people of Cuba who depend on the refinery for jobs, or are helped because of the revenue generated would have been the losers, not the Castro government or the U.S. government. Hell, they'll go on, one factory more or less won't be the end of the world for them. Shit, Fidel will make the destruction or saving of the structure a political show piece. It's just a matter of altering his speech a bit."

The boat followed southeast along the coast away from the direction of Havana. We pulled into an inlet and were hustled into a truck and moved inland a few miles to a cabin where we were to clean up, change clothes and eat. Our instructions for escape would come then.

When I came out of the bathroom towards the dining table, there were several people in the room. I asked who they were. One fellow said he was Carlo Romeo, working with my government to help.

Joyce came out and began talking to the men. Carlo and I were going over our escape route out of Cuba and exchanging some information. It seemed like we talked forever and went over and over the plans. He then told me who would be meeting me and I was startled. I couldn't imagine the people he referred to being a party to a homosexual partnership for international cooperation. I was tired and needed to clear my head for a minute.

I settled down on the couch to talk and relax. Joyce looked remarkable all dressed up and clean.

"Stephen, the experience has changed you a bit." She smiled.

"More dashing and romantic."

"Yes, but that's not what I mean."

"What do you mean "looking up at her?

"You're not so much of a smart ass with your remarks as you were a week ago."

"I'm out of my environment. Just wait till we get back to civilization."

"I don't think so. You've been mellowing all week."

"You're correct. "Laughing to myself as she rubbed my hair, The week had taken a rather stiff toll of my otherwise satirical posture. "We're not out of this yet, we still have to get off the island and home; home for me, your potentially new adopted home."

"Carlo seems positive about the plan to get us out of here. I feel rather safe with them."

"Oh yes, I can see why."

"Don't be like that Steve."

"I was just having fun with you!" I patted her on the arm to calm her. She seemed defensive.

"We should get some rest. We leave early in the morning."

I looked over at her "It's early now. You mean a nap and we're off."

Just as Joyce stretched out on the sofa and I on the floor beside her, it seemed like Carlo and company came into the room again. They felt bad about the primitive conditions. We tried to explain that after the last week's activities, this seemed like a five star hotel.

Then Carlo agreed, and this bothered me. "What do you mean you agree -- how do you know where we were?"

"We don't know your every action, but we were aware of your movements. Kept track as best we could, and reported them to your government's representatives in Washington. I'm afraid I am not at liberty to disclose with whom I spoke. Quite frankly, I'm not sure who I really do have the cooperative arrangement with. It was all very clandestine, you know."

"You have a distant smile, Steve?"

"Oh - its okay, Joyce. I was reflecting on what Carlo said."

Turning to him "Why didn't you help us earlier?"

"I'll tell you what I said to your little spy group in the U.S. -- why in the devil should my friends and I risk our already dreadful existence for two people with nothing to gain? I mean, we have life difficult enough without any public display of insurrection."

"He's correct, Steve. Life is hell for them here."

"Okay, let's say we're happy you decided to help at this time. One more time explain how we get to Miami?"

Chapter 15
ON THE SCENE - BACK AT THE SCENE - BEHIND THE SCENE

Arthur helped put Simon's body in the boat. The crew was part of the unique gay underground organization Arthur was sent to organize. On the other side of the refinery a crowd was beginning to form and the lights from the refinery were being shown toward the dock. There was little time to lose. They had to shove off. Fortunately, it was dark to hide their escape route, which was in the opposite direction from that of Masters and Hurtado.

"What the hell is that ahead of us, Arthur?" asked one of the crew.

"It's too dark to tell yet. Pull up closer. It may be a fish. It went under -- no wait, it's a person swimming. How dam close to the shore are we? Where could he be swimming?"

"We're about 100 yards from shore, Arthur, and there is a pile of rocks to our right another 100 yards or so."

"It must be one of Dante's men trying to get away. Pick him up. We'll give him some of his own medicine for questioning that we received in the cave.

"Is this to be your sweet revenge scene, Arty? He went under! I don't think he can stay down long. He has got to be tired. There he is - smack him with the emergency oar."

Arthur had a smile of a man awaiting revenge. "Help me pull him up men. He's heavy. What! Who is this - oh, oh, - who do we have here? Yup!"

"Good Lord, Arthur, its Perez Guerra, one of Dante's top leaders. He's the one who commanded the plane job that brought Masters here."

"The son-of-a-bitch will talk later or be turned over to the authorities. Maybe both. Tie him up and let's get the hell out of here."

Dante Perez stood on the hill staring in disbelief at the retreat of men. The approaching vehicles blocked an easy exit out the road. But that was planned for. Only, he didn't think it would have been necessary. The assault was not supposed to have met any resistance. Especially from his ex-prisoners. It was sloppy, he knew it. But revolutionary groups, no matter how hard they work, can't equal the total regimentation of the armed forces. Maybe it's the equipment, facilities and weapons they have, Could be the group as a whole is better trained. He hated it when anything went wrong and envied the precision of crack troops.

"Dante, Perez Guerra is not here. I saw him head toward the water. He must be going down the shore line and then to the meeting place."

"Is the other American in place as near the site as possible?" Dante asked.

"Yes, and our men are away from the scene. We must go now. Lights from the road, it must be troops."

"Goddamn those people - how could this have happened? Is the jeep ready?" Dante had the look of a confused and mad general. "Si."

"Let's go. You're right. Is Juan dead?"

"Si. We have his body Dante. The authorities know him. We took those who they might know and left the others with the American."

"Dante, how will they believe two old guards could have done all this?"

"It's not necessary with the dead CIA man, Johnson. Besides, Fidel is so eloquent he will make heroes out of them. Even though there will be many unanswered questions."

"Is it enough, Dante?"

"My loyal friend, I don't know. We can only hope. Either way, we must still try and regroup to hit the conference in Miami."

"I thought Perez Guerra was to be a part of that plan."

"He was. Maybe you will lead that mission for us. If you don't kill us with your crazy driving."

"Sorry, this cross field escape is rough."

"I know. I'm upset. We must get Jose' Francia out of jail and back with us. We have only a few days till Miami. We must travel all night to be at the main meeting place. This disruption could mean problems

if discipline and order are not
quickly established. My friend,
groups like ours can break apart
easily Discouragement,
disenchantment with goals or minor
setbacks can cost us valued members.
The problems then come with those
who have left."

"Why?"

"Because they sell their
information to the government. Fidel
had these problems, as has every
revolutionary movement."

-------------- ---------------

"Inform the rest of the research
council that we have heard from Cuba
and our dynamic duo are safe and
should be leaving for pickup
tomorrow."

"Yes, Mr. Jamison."

Robert Jamison looked at John Greyson and smiled very slightly. "I thought we had lost a good research aide."

"The news from Harrington was a relief. He's still operating in Cuba, for both groups, CIA and our needs."

"Our needs are minimal, John. We only enter in to try and keep the red, white and blue from getting black eyes or red faces. Although, despite our best efforts, we don't seem to fare well. It would be nice if we could do the front work instead of leaping in at the end to spread lime on shit so it won't smell."

John looked, smiled and said "Wouldn't our faces have been red if Masters had been found out -- especially when this wasn't his assignment."

"He's now field qualified John - if he lives. Who took his research in Miami?"

"That's another point of the Harrington message, Robert. Masters reports a possible political setup at the conference on Key Biscayne. Which was to be his ultimate job of seeing some clumsy politicians didn't stuff both feet in their mouths. Now it appears he wants the FBI notified to string security tight."

"Looks like he'll be involved after all, although his involvement was set up perfectly by the labor conference on Miami Beach. Some of our beloved politicians are itching to make some statements about the treatment of workers in Poland and supervision of workers' rights. Masters was to be introduced on the scene to settle down the group with facts and remain an interested onlooker to the conference. I've taken the liberty to pass on the potential trouble possibility, Robert."

"Fine. What about the pickup, John? It's not our policy to make cloak and dagger rescues. Can't CIA handle this officially?"

"Yes, thanks to Harrington's involvement. But, after Masters and Hurtado are ready for movement back to Washington, you may wish to be involved." John looked over to the tall and stately figure who displayed a half smile and a perplexed stare at the same time.

"Certainly. I'll be on that flight with them. This affair has gotten so damn much publicity. Masters is an arrogant fellow to begin with. This can only make him more difficult to deal with."

"Most of the agents we use are prima donnas, Robert, Hell, they all are brilliant, well-educated people. As a group, they're less disciplined and structured than the normal run of society and a damn far cry from the paramilitary stereotype we use at the CIA."

"John, I'm not an expert on the area, but your message mentions a

Bahama rescue. There are 700 islands, 2000 inlets, and over 750 miles involved here."

"Don't worry, Robert, we only use a couple for this sort of thing - Harrington knows. Besides, only about 50 or 75 of the 700 are inhabited. The real trick will be getting them off Cuba and away from the military. I don't know how they'll accomplish that, but we'll be ready to assist."

"What do we do with Masters' travel partner?"

"That we will discuss at committee, Robert."

"The options are not positive. If we keep her, it's an international incident. If we give her back, she may be short on life expectancy. John, I think we should do some checking to see about the official position of the Havana government concerning her. If it looks negative, we may find her a new home in Canada or elsewhere."

"Will they want to see her when they land in D.C.?"

"I don't know, I assume they don't know about their escape from Dante Perez. It complicates matters that they have to escape from Cuba to begin with."

"Excuse me gentlemen. The Admiral awaits you both in the meeting room."

"Thank you." The young security assistant exited the room after delivering the message.

"The Admiral? Did you know he was coming today, John?"

"Hell, no!"

Both turned and walked in. The Admiral was pacing the floor. "John, Robert, what the Sam Hill is Masters and that Cuban broad up to?"

"Our information is they are ready to leave the island, Admiral."

"Well you didn't get all the news for once. Navy intelligence got us this one."

"One what? Will you stop playing this game?" Stated John with some disdain in his voice.

"Well," the Admiral began, "it appears there was some damn raid on a sugar factory or whatever the hell they call them in Cuba."

"They're called refineries the world around, Admiral." John sharply chimed in.

"What does that have to do with Masters?" Robert asked, the wrinkles around his eyes deepened with concern over the possibilities.

"I'm not sure, but they found a dead military intelligence man at the site. Yes, John, he's Navy. We didn't send him to blow up any sugar factory. His name was Johnson."

"Why the hell are you sending people there without letting the CIA know?"

"John, Jesus Christ - everyone has people in Cuba. Half the fucking island is made up of spies from around the world. The Castro government depends on them for a balanced trade account."

"Gentlemen, please" Robert interrupted to act as mediator, "let's settle the problem of getting our research man and Joyce back first. Go on Admiral."

"The Castro government is hopping mad. They're going to have a big, big rally to expose this as another mini Bay of Pigs that was stopped by some heroic night guards or some crap like that."

"Oh boy, another Six hour marathon speech by Fidel. I'm getting a headache. I can't believe we are in the middle of this whole damn mess. What is the connection to Masters and Hurtado?" Robert hit the table with a pencil.

"Well, from what we learned, those two were pinpointed as CIA spies to help arrange the destruction of this prize sugar factory - refinery - excuse me, John. The destruction of which would hurt the economy of Cuba."

"Robert, that helps clear up the problem of what to do with Hurtado. Home coming is not an option." John smiled.

"You asked for me, Mr. Johnson?" The aide entered the room.

"Yes, will you get us some brandy please?"

"Yes, sir."

"Has the White House been notified, Admiral?"

"Yes, Robert."

"That means I'll be going there shortly. I may never sleep today."

"I don't mean to make yours and Johnson's evening any worse; but, getting out of Cuba will be harder than ever now. Catching those two will be the crowning evidence of a massive U.S. plot." The old Admiral leaned back in his chair and lit a cigar.

"Drink up gentlemen, the next few hours are going to seem like an eternity. John, I want to be notified immediately of their arrival in the Bahamas. I will have a plane ready to go and pick them up at Nassau."

"When do we notify the press, Robert?"

"I don't know, John, let's see
what the White House has in mind.
Since this has grown to a full blown
incident, the official State
Department position will need be
taken into account."

Chapter 16
THE GET-A-WAY

It was barely light over the horizon and the humidity was already high. Whatever happened to those ocean breezes that are supposed to keep Cuba from seeming like a steam bath? Carlo came in with Arthur Harrington. My state of shock of seeing him must have shown on my face.

"Surprised to see me again, but I had to get back to help with getting you off the island."

I looked at Arthur. He was not in the best of shape from the confinement. I wondered what he could do now.

Joyce stared for a second and asked "Why?" What happened to the old plan that didn't involve him?

"Things have gotten 'hot' so to speak for you two. It makes the search for the hijack recovery seem like a Boy Scout attempt."

Arthur flopped down on to the couch and held his head for a moment.

"Listen, things are going to be tough getting you out of here. Between boat patrols, search planes and almost a complete examination of the island no stone is unturned."

"Jesus, Arthur, we weren't going to just leave by a scheduled airline before", I said, "What the hell is the difference?"

"There was a dead American at the site of the refinery." Arthur began. "You remember Johnson I told you about?"

"Yes, he died in the cave didn't he?"

"It doesn't matter, he was placed at the refinery as leading the based CIA attack and you and Joyce are figured as heading the plot to ruin Cuba's successful international sugar et al trade."

"You're wrong Arthur," Joyce interrupted, "You said Johnson was Navy intelligence not CIA."

Carlo smiled and said "It's all the same sweet stuff. American spies plus a Cuban traitor. They want you both very bad."

"This plan," Arthur began, "is more adventuresome, but it can work."

"I like it already."

"Quiet, Steve," Joyce threw an elbow into my side.

Arthur stared with a smile at the both of us. He looked like he could use a long vacation. But all these undercover types have that same look of desperation and fatigue.

Arthur raised his hands to get our attention and started again to describe our exit from the island.

"Do you remember the soldier chap involved in the cult ritual?"

"Yes." Joyce answered.

"Well, he is going to be in on this as our official military lingo fellow."

"How did you find and convince him?"

"Don't worry about it Masters, just be glad he's grateful and consented to help. We need a military person because we're getting out of here by stealing a patrol boat and heading for the outer islands of the Bahama Chain. A helicopter will intercept on the way to finish the trip for you. We'll need him to make our movements seem legitimate."

"I don't know Arthur. That seems like a plot out of an old Dean Martin comedy spy movie. You just don't steal patrol boats." I got up and walked toward Carlo and asked if he had a better idea. He laughed and told me it would be okay and ignored my grimace.

Arthur stood and motioned for us to leave. He would explain the rest on the way to the boat. We needed to be there before it got much lighter. The spot was east of Matanzas where the boat hijack was to take place.

We walked out the door of the quaint little cabin and looked around. We were motioned to a truck by Carlo that was parked in front of the cabin. The truck was loaded with fruits and vegetables to serve as a decoy. The arrangement was not an unusual site on Cuban roads. Just as it was not an unusual site on roads in many parts of the United States. Food has to get to market.

The arrangement of fruit boxes reminded me a little of the boxcar a few days earlier when we hid from the authorities. The truck was like a large pick-em-up made in Europe by the consortium of common market manufacturers. It was a small mid-size flatbed. The crates were stacked three high except for a hole in the center about two crates square. Between the second and third level of crates, two boards were placed that would support another crate on top to form the third level. Each board was in the middle of the crate leaving enough room for us to slide be- tween to get in the open spot below.

It took some convincing by the group to get me down there. I just knew there would be a tarantula hiding in the fruit. The fruit and vegetables were wet for some reason unknown to me. That smell came back to me of a rotten salad. I spent some time in Panama in my early years. When it would rain or be damp, the vegetation took on the smell of a partially rotten salad. It would be tough to sit out the trip with that aroma. Joyce didn't seem to mind the smell and told me to shut up and be happy we had a ride and were getting out alive. I tried to caution her that we weren't out and in one piece yet.

Unfortunately, this journey would take us in the direction of the refinery. In fact, on the road in front of the field where I set fire to the piles of brush.

It seemed like an eternity that we sat back among the crates, then we slowed down and I could hear Carlo yell for us to take a peek.

As we lifted a crate out of the way and eased our heads above, the reason was obvious. There across the field were soldiers and people combing the area around the refinery.

Carlo yelled for us to get back down so as not to arouse suspicion. The truck started out again. We bumped and jolted for another fifteen or twenty minutes.

Again the truck stopped. I assumed it was for us to take another peek. So both hands grabbed a crate and I yelled, "What the hell do we see now?"

Instead of the jovial response expected from Arthur or Carlo, I got a message indirectly. As the crate went up, what seemed only a fraction of a second, Arthur was jumping down to join us. There wasn't much room in the crate hole hiding area to begin with. Now it was ridiculous. The initial position was my face in his armpit.

Arthur whispered for us to be quiet because we were at a police check point. He was back there just to avoid too many questions. I not only remained quiet, but my breathing stopped until the truck moved. The check only appeared to involve rattling some of the crates and looking under the truck, from what Spanish could be understood by me.

As the truck began moving, we all breathed more easily. Arthur would just stay there since the trip to our destination was not long. And, why take added risks of him moving about above the crates to get to the truck cab.

The sun was now beginning to take its place just above the horizon. Carlo and another of his men helped us out of the hiding place. We wouldn't be back for the truck, so it needed to be hidden from sight.

My idea was to cover it with brush. Joyce smiled "We don't have time to dig up half of the area's foliage to heap it all over a truck."

Arthur interrupted with a fine idea. "We're going to park it off the road in the field, take off a tire and block it to make it appear as if we had some mechanical trouble."

The idea was simple, yet very clever. We did that, with more sweat than the idea conjured up. I didn't realize blocking up a truck was that hard?

We began the walk to the boat location. On the other side of the field, west and north from the truck stopping place, was the marina. We approached the area that resembled a small marina back on the eastern shore of Delaware. The patrol and fishing boats used it for fuel, eating, and there was some minor repair work done. I assumed this by

the scant number of boats dry-docked
behind the boat house which was
about fifty yards east of the
restaurant type building. The
restaurant-looking building was at
the edge of the pier. The pier
jutted out into the water and the
boats would pull up alongside for
fuel. More permanent dock facilities
for overnight or whatever were to
the west side of the fuel pier.

We were just on the west edge of
the lot behind the restaurant
building. Arthur pointed out our
soldier friend at the first pump
area on the west side of the pier.
He was talking with the crew of a
patrol boat. The boat looked like
the kind people charter to go deep
sea fishing. Only it was drab gray
with guns mounted instead of fishing

poles. There was only a three man crew. The soldier was directing the crew toward the restaurant building and walking with them. In the back of the building, there were toilet facilities. Good old mother nature and her inevitable calling to urinate. As the crew entered the bathroom facility, we moved quickly.

One of Carlo's people was filling the boat with fuel. We headed toward the toilet. As the first soldier came out of the toilet he smiled at Joyce. At least his last vision on earth was to be pleasant. Arthur flipped a wire around his neck and slit his throat. He was dead in an instant. The other men with us quickly took off his clothes for us to wear before they got too bloody. The second man came out and met a similar fate and I heard a thump inside the toilet. All three were dead quickly.

Arthur, myself, and Joyce stripped quickly and put on the uniforms. The fit wasn't perfect, especially for Joyce. It would be adequate if someone looked at us through binoculars. Carlo and company would dispose of the bodies.

We got on the boat. Joyce smiled and asked how she looked. "I didn't think vanity was a socialist concern." I patted her on the rear and helped her to a seat.

"You did raise my blood pressure during the change. Why didn't you wear a bra or something?"

"I don't think I had any effect on Arthur, Carlo or his men.

"With a big smile on my face, "I must agree with you there."

My undergarments were filthy. It felt cleaner without any. I didn't know it would be a public change of clothes.

The soldier started the boat. Fortunately it was still early and no other boats were at the pier. To our surprise the whole plan actually went off as Arthur predicted.

Arthur came to where Joyce and I were sitting and began some explanation of what was to transpire from this point.

"Listen, our soldier friend knows the patrol route this craft is to follow from the conversation with the original crew. We will follow it for an hour or so till we alter our

heading to intercept with the
helicopter. To make this look
official, Joyce will man the rear
guns, you're up front and we'll
follow the original crew orders. We
are going to be passed by another
patrol boat returning in a half
hour. If all goes well we signal and
keep going. Any trouble and we will
have to take the other boat."

I took my position up front. It
was going to be a nice sunny day, As
the boat picked up speed, the front
end rose and the ride was disturbed
only by the slight pounding of waves
hitting the bow. The mist felt
refreshing. My heart was still
thumping and probably would not slow
down till we were safe. Even then I
wondered if it would ever go back to
normal speed after the last days. To

have my stomach out of my mouth and back where it belonged would be delightful. God, what I wouldn't do for a pack of Rolaids.

Arthur sighted the other patrol boat and alerted us to be ready. The boats approached each other and slowed down not 20 yards apart. We signaled what I prayed would be a correct response.

Out of nervous tension, I kept the binoculars to my eyes and looking over the horizon. One begins to think of all the things which could go wrong like Joyce's hat could blow off and that lovely hair would come tumbling down. Another reason to hold binoculars was to keep a tight hold of my own hat and hide the light color hair from view.

The exchange of signals ended and it seemed like an eternity we sat floating across from each other. We hit the throttle and took off as did the other craft. The surge of excitement was felt through my whole body. We pulled it off. They didn't recognize us.

The next half hour passed slowly before we altered course. It was at this point the regional patrol boat was to alter course and circle back much closer to the shore line. This was still a dangerous point in the escape plan.

Our boat was still not that far from Cuba, only an hour away literally from where this all began.

This was a serious line of thought. How was Arthur and Boy Wonder going to get back? Did this craft carry that much fuel? I posed the questions to Arthur. His answer was the expected professional response. Worry about my own part of this mission and its success. The other part was his responsibility. He would worry about its success. We exchanged warm smiles and a hand shake.

"Why don't you and Joyce go down below and get some sleep, Things are going to pick up when your ride comes."

Joyce looked confused at Arthur's comment. He clarified, "Sweet stuff, you may not be in any danger, but everyone from the top down is going to be questioning you

Plus, there is still the possible problem in Miami at the conference on Key Biscayne to check out."

Down below was small. A cooking area immediately at the foot of the stairs and what appeared like a giant shelf fora bed. If one were claustrophobic, the accommodations would not be comfortable. However, fatigue conquers a lot of otherwise difficult situations.

"Hungry, Steve?" Joyce asked while standing at the cooking equipment.

"No. Come here, we need some rest."

"Rest - I know you better, remember. Your perverted little mind is now trying to figure some possible configuration on this bed to make love and not be bounced on top of the stove."

"American ingenuity will prevail." Joyce crawled up beside me and gave me a tender kiss.

"Your American ingenuity can't solve the problem of Cuban fatigue. Let's sleep."

We were both awakened by Arthur's banging on a pot with a spoon and yelling to get ready for the transfer. "Come on you two...it's time to move, your ride is coming."

I couldn't believe it. "Are you sure?"

"No, it may be someone else's helicopter meeting us in the middle of nowhere. Damn politicians are all alike."

"Joyce gave Arthur a hug and kiss on the cheek. "Can't you come with us?

You may not get back alive? Oh, please, Arthur." "We all have our jobs to do dear girl. But mine is still in Cuba. Get the hell up there, sweet stuff."

I couldn't resist asking. "Arthur, why have you taken to calling her sweet stuff lately? You didn't when we first met and began all this at the cave."

"There was a time my boy...there was a time when things were different. Joyce reminds me of those times."

The years in Arthur's type of work were beginning to show. His dark hair was turning gray and lines were starting to form around the eyes and forehead. "You know, my friend." looking directly at him, "men in their late forties can get hurt in your line of work." I gave Arthur a hug and thanked him for his help. We would transmit the information about Key Biscayne through the Research Institute via Robert Jamison.

The helicopter had dropped the hoist and Joyce was beginning her lift to safety. Arthur asked "She doesn't know yet about your other line of work?"

"No, she believes me to be a rather smug politician. I figured you found out when I heard Carlo talk before. I might add it surprised me the connection between

Carlo and my employer was mentioned."

"She'll figure it out before long. I imagine your boss will be meeting you in the Bahamas. .You were to go originally to an island and be picked up there. But that changed with Johnson being at the scene of the refinery. You'll now go straight to the airfield and then by jet home to the U.S."

"Only after considerable debriefing." I laughed and shook his hand again and went up via the hoist.

As we gained elevation in the helicopter, I looked out over the horizon and I shook with fear for Arthur. Another boat was approaching. "Hey, look! Can we go down and render some assistance?" I yelled to the pilot.

"Sorry sir, my orders are to get you both back right away with no delays."

Joyce yelled, "It could be trouble for him to explain this. He may be killed."

"Sorry, but if we go to help, there will be planes called in from Cuba, if they're not already. We have to keep heading out of here and fast."

Joyce and I watched as long as possible. My thoughts reflected over the help he gave us. Professionals in the field were not to be sentimental about such things as saving another person's life. We could only hope the soldier and

Arthur would head back the opposite way and be safe. If there is such a thing as safety for a gay undercover agent in Cuba.

------------------- ----------

The copter settled down at the landing field and we were ushered from it and directed to an awaiting jet. The smiling faces of cloak and dagger type people have a certain melodious ring about them. It is difficult to tell if it's one of joy or just part of their training.

As we boarded the jet, Robert Jamison grabbed me by the hand and pulled me down on the seat next to him. The seating arrangement was like a booth, only with individual captain's chairs and a table in the middle that had a video screen and radio mechanism built into the center. He then began to yell "What in the hell were you involved with? Jesus - do you have any idea of the diplomatic fracas that's going on? Hell, the White House has been chewing my head off. They think we sent you to Cuba...Somehow, the hijack was a front. Christ, I had a time explaining that part was real...but all this other shit!"

John Greyson was across the table from us and interrupted. "Damnit man, do you know what a black eye this will be for the CIA...and we aren't involved?"

I stood up, smiled, and took Joyce by the hand "Robert Jamison, John Greyson, I would like you to meet Joyce Hurtado, former Cuban diplomat, who can collaborate whatever I tell you!"

"Gentlemen," I began, "there is some unfinished business that may involve our going direct to Miami. Please listen to this first. We will then explain everything in detail." I leaned back in my chair to catch my breath and organize the story into some logical order. To my surprise, Joyce began to tell the story about the potential Key Biscayne problem. It wasn't just the telling of the story. She knew John Greyson. You can tell by how people relate to each other in body language and all.

"Joyce, excuse me for interrupting, but....

John Greyson interrupted. "Joyce works for us - CIA...we recruited her at Penn State. Or sort of recruited her. She is still very loyal to Cuba. Just not to Fidel or the Russians. A devout socialist and feminist and wanting her country's independence."

I looked at Robert, "Did you know this?"

"How in the hell am I supposed to know every operative in the field, Masters?"

I looked at Joyce and smiled. She spoke up, "Well my dear, you didn't volunteer to tell my anything about your 'activities' or whatever."

I answered, "You're correct, I should have figured it out when you clubbed the fellow during the escape. However, I am not a CIA representative. My affiliation is on a. higher and more philosophical plain. A sort of trouble shooter behind the scenes

"The way you fight it was obvious that you weren't a soldier."

"Very good Joyce," Robert smiled. "Masters can be a real difficult person at times."

"Robert," I asked. "How can you switch from sounding so dignified one moment to something reminiscent of a drill sergeant the next?"

"Practice. It takes years of training in Washington trenches to get this way. You did say there was something important.. And, Joyce was filling us in before you became dumbfounded and interrupted."

Joyce began where she left off before to complete the story of the counter part of the plan to disrupt the Key. Biscayne conference and make it seem like a Cuban reprisal.

Robert looked at us both and began. "We got your earlier message about this possibility and began to take security steps. We wanted to hear it from you both to be sure our information is correct. I think the problem may be settled."

"How is it settled Robert?" we asked.

He began. 'The Navy intercepted a boat with some of Dante's men and a dead Cuban officer on board. Dante was not there. He may still attempt to disrupt the conference, but we doubt such a thing will be tried now. Plus, our sources in Cuba report Perez Guerra is reported captured by Cuban authorities."

It felt like the weight of the world went off my shoulders. It was just about over. All except for some debriefing and press interviews. "Oh Robert, I hope you brought a change of clothes for us. We could use a shower and a drink."

"I agree, you do need a shower, Masters. Be my guests."

Robert Jamison sat up and called for our attention. "Okay, we will be landing in about ten minutes. There is a press area set up for you both.

When that is over, there will be a driver to take you to your hotel. Our next meeting will be tomorrow morning at 10:00 A.M., if that is okay with you, Mr. Masters - Ms. Hurtado?"

"Yes, that's fine. I was afraid you might suggest some ridiculous earlier hour. This meeting will not involve Ms. Hurtado, I presume."

"It certainly will, Mr. Masters. There are a host of officials who must speak to you both. Plus, we must decide what to do with Joyce. Her country is demanding her immediate return." Robert paused to take a sip of brandy. "Plus, there is the Key Biscayne item we must account for. Well give me your answer."

I looked at Jamison and nodded.

"A curt smile and tipping your drink is hardly the response I expected from a sophisticated person, Mr. Masters."

"My thoughts were on what nice restaurant I might take Joyce to for dinner. A sort of victory celebration and fond goodbye. I doubt that a Cuban representative will ever again show up in Harrisburg; despite our lovely Harris Town renovations."

"You never know, I am a Penn State football fan. I do hate to watch games by myself. We might --"

"Quiet, both of you, there is an excited press who wants to know every aspect of the hijacking and the rather wild escape from your captors. Remember how we practiced your answers so there are no political repercussions. After you both have been completely debriefed again tomorrow, more exhaustive interviews can be scheduled. But for now, stick to the versions agreed to."

"Certainly, Mr. Jamison. God knows we wouldn't want to upset the diplomatic corps. Joyce, I will call for you about 8:00 P.M. There is a nice Italian restaurant in downtown D.C., just off Connecticut Avenue, where they let you take forever to eat. And, it's only a short walk to the Hilton Piano Bar. I need a slow quiet pace for a little while yet."

Joyce looked up, "I thought we agreed during our week together to share in decision making. The

Italian restaurant is fine, but there's a nice dancing lounge down the street from it that sounds like fun; then followed up by a nightcap at the Hilton."

Robert Jamison seemed delighted by Joyce's response and quipped, "Well, Masters, let me tip my glass to the young lady. I didn't realize the positive feminine attitude had invaded Cuba. She seems like a suitable match for you."

Joyce smiled and couldn't resist the temptation for one more little political remark. "Mr. Jamison, the socialist political ideology has fostered the equality of women from the beginning. It's not just a political fantasy or rich white women's pastime

For us."

I showed up for my meeting at
9:55 A.M., awake, alert and ready to
go into exhaustive detail. As
expected, Mr. Jamison was there with
a recorder and stenographer. I
couldn't figure out if he didn't
trust technology, was that
fastidious, or if it was another
silly requirement. Being Secretary
of Labor had taught me much of silly
bureaucracy despite my short tenure
in the office. In addition, there
were other persons from various
government agencies. Some of the
agencies present were covert in
nature, others purely political, or
like my own representatives from

Pennsylvania. It would be a long drawn out process, but necessary.

Robert pulled me aside during the session and explained that there was a lot of pressure building to send Joyce back to Cuba. Since we were so skilled at escapes, why don't we try one at the lunch break?

They had debriefed us both. All that was going on now was trying to figure a plan to appease the anger of the Castro government. The way might be to give up Hurtado.

Joyce and I went out the front door of the room and walked down the hallway toward the employee cafeteria acting as if we belonged there and not drawing undue attention. We slopped around the food trays and walked hunched behind the counter to the kitchen.

John Greyson was waiting in the kitchen area and took us via a car to a waiting helicopter. I asked if this was a CIA trip or our own group. He smiled. The CIA was out. I knew where we would end up. It was sort of fitting----he was taking us to the remote Bahama Island the CIA uses for various aspects of its Caribbean operations—including R&R.

It was our original escape plan destination from Cuba and it became a second escape from Cuba for Joyce. It has beautiful white sand and the clearest water imaginable. Certainly the best prescription to rest and regain our energy. It would also allow time to get Joyce a new identity and assess the damage to my own double identity. But, the most important point was we would be the only two people on the island!!

Made in the USA
Middletown, DE
02 April 2018